DOCTOR WHO AND THE UNDERWORLD

Based on the BBC television serial by Bob Baker and Dave Martin by arrangement with the British Broadcasting Corporation

TERRANCE DICKS

Number 67
in the
Doctor Who Library

A TARGET BOOK

published by
the Paperback Division of
W. H. ALLEN & Co. Ltd

A Target Book

Published in 1980
by the Paperback Division of W.H. Allen & Co. Ltd
A Howard & Wyndham Company
44 Hill Street, London W1X 8LB

Reprinted 1980
Reprinted 1982
Réprinted 1984

Novelisation copyright © 1980 by Terrance Dicks
Original script copyright © 1978 by Bob Baker and Dave Martin
'Doctor Who' series copyright © 1978, 1980 by the
British Broadcasting Corporation

Printed in Great Britain by
Hunt Barnard Printing Ltd, Aylesbury, Bucks.

ISBN 0 426 20068 3

Contents

Prologue

Once there were the Minyans.

A humanoid race on an Earth-like planet in a galaxy on the far side of the Universe.

Like Man, the Minyans learned the use of tools and weapons. Like Man, they changed from hunters to farmers, built villages, banded into tribes, threw up leaders and wise men. They started the long hard climb that leads all intelligent life-forms to civilisation, technology, and at last to the stars.

On a planet called Gallifrey there were the Time Lords, a people far advanced in power and wisdom. They had already conquered Time and Space, and were exploring the galaxies around them.

They landed on Minyos and studied the planet and its people. With the best possible intentions, they decided to play god.

The results were catastrophic.

Not at first, of course. The Time Lords made themselves known to the Minyans, who promptly began to worship them. The kindly space gods began conferring the benefits of science upon them. They taught them the beginnings of medicine, introduced the wheel, the plough, steam-power, the internal combustion engine. They altered the structure of Minyan society to accelerate their development.

The Minyans were a bright, aggressive race. They learned their new lessons with astonishing speed. In a few short generations they raced up the ladder of progress until they reached the level of atomic-powered civilisation. Soon they had mastered space flight and began to explore the planets around them.

Their teachers watched the Minyans' progress with self-satisfied approval. They even passed on the precious secret of bodily regeneration, so that selected astronauts could make the long voyages between the stars.

All in all, the Time Lords thought their experiments a great success—until Minyan mobs surrounded their bases and began killing Time Lords.

Benevolent dictators, worshipped as gods, the Time Lords had ruled Minyos for hundreds of years. What they failed to realise was that for every Minyan who worshipped them, there were a dozen who feared and hated them. A resistance movement had begun, with the slogan, 'Free Minyos!' Over the generations it grew and grew, until one day it erupted in revolution. All over the planet, Minyans appeared at Time Lord bases, with the new shield guns in their hands.

So sudden and savage was the attack that most of the Time Lords on the planet were killed. Only a handful escaped to Gallifrey where the High Council met for an agonised post-mortem.

It is greatly to the credit of the Time Lords that there was never any question of revenge. Even then, they had powers at their disposal which could have destroyed the planet with ease. But they were a moral race, and they realised that the catastrophe was largely of their own making. They had learned a bitter and painful lesson.

'Besides,' said the President of the Council sadly, 'it is neither fitting nor necessary that we should destroy the Minyans. In the fullness of time, they will surely destroy themselves.'

The prophecy was very soon fulfilled. After the expulsion of the Time Lords, the Minyans began warring amongst themselves. Thanks to the Time Lords, the wars were fought not with swords and spears but with atomic missiles.

They destroyed their planet.

One black day a Junior Time Lord on scanning duty in the Temporal Control Room made a routine check on Minyos and found it no longer existed. It had been fragmented by a series of colossal atomic explosions. A scattering of radioactive asteroids occupied the space where once there had been a world.

The effect on the Time Lords was shattering. With the death of a planet on their consciences, they developed a policy of non-intervention. Their curiosity was too great to confine themselves to Gallifrey. They would continue their quest for knowledge, continue to study the inhabited planets of the Universe. But in future they would only observe and record. They would never, never interfere.

(Non-intervention remained official Time Lord policy, though later it was modified under the influence of a renegade Time Lord known as the Doctor.)

But Minyos was not dead, not completely. In the years before the holocaust, a few far-sighted Minyans had sought means of escaping the coming disaster. They had developed a mind-pacifier, though too late to end the wars. They had sent out hastily constructed scout ships, and had actually found a habitable world in a solar system close to their own. They established a tiny colony on this world, which they had christened Minyos II. They had gathered the genetic heritage of Minyos into a Race Bank, and despatched it to Minyos II in a space ship called the P7E.

The P7E was never to reach Minyos II. A failure in its guidance systems sent it far off course. It vanished, somewhere in the colossal turbulence at the edge of creation. Faint signals were picked up from its automatic distress beacon. They faded and died.

The scientists of Minyos staked everything on one last gamble. Straining the resources of their dying planet, they built an Interstellar Patrol Vessel, a massively powerful craft designed for an eternal voyage. They equipped it with perpetual energy-generators, with re-cycling and regeneration equipment, chose the finest and most dedicated astronauts on Minyos for its crew.

During the final days of Minyos, the Interstellar Patrol Vessel blasted off on its vital mission—to find the lost P7E and bring the Race Bank safely to Minyos II.

Soon after the ship blasted off, the planet blasted itself from existence.

In the endless years that followed the little colony on Minyos II waited for a ship that never came. With the Race Bank, it could create a new Minyan race, people the planet and re-create the world that had been destroyed. Without it, it could do little more than survive.

The Interstellar Patrol Vessel roamed the turbulent frontiers of creation, endlessly searching for the ship that held the survival of the Minyan race.

A hundred thousand years went by.

Then one day, the Minyans crossed the path of the Time Lords once again. Or rather, that of one particular Time Lord.

A renegade known as the Doctor ...

Chapter One

The Nebula

It was the edge of creation.

Even the expanding Universe must have a frontier, and this was it. An area of incredible turbulence, where stars, planets, whole galaxies flamed into existence in the twinkling of a cosmic eye.

Through this howling chaos there moved a mystery. It was small and square and blue with a flashing light on top. Strange symbols were written above the door. Two words in one of the languages of an immeasurably distant planet called Earth—'Police Box'.

The police box was not a police box at all, but a space/time craft called the TARDIS. Inside its incredibly large control room was a girl. She was tall and strong: she wore a brief animal-skin costume and a heavy fighting knife.

The girl's name was Leela, and she was the companion of a traveller in Time and Space known as the Doctor. Leela had grown up in a tribe that lived by perpetual warfare. She joined the Doctor in search of excitement, and found herself involved in a series of adventures more terrifying than she could ever have imagined.

Leela was quick-witted and resourceful, and she had

soon adapted herself to her new life. But some things still baffled her. One of them was the TARDIS itself.

To begin with, there was its shape. The Doctor had explained that it looked like something called a 'police box'. As far as Leela could understand, this was a device for summoning the city guards in a town called London, on the planet Earth.

(She had once visited London with the Doctor, but there had been no other police boxes about. The Doctor explained they hadn't been invented yet.)

The TARDIS was shaped like a police box because something called the 'chameleon mechanism' had got stuck. It was supposed to enable the TARDIS to blend with its surroundings. But now it was jammed, so the TARDIS remained in the shape of a police box on planets where police boxes, policemen, or even human beings were completely unknown.

Then there was its size. From the outside it was only big enough to hold one, or at most two people. Yet inside it held not only the control room in which she was now standing, but an apparently infinite number of rooms, passages, chambers, corridors of every shape and size.

The heart of the TARDIS was the many-sided central control console which Leela was now regarding nervously. The Doctor habitually spoke to the TARDIS as if it were alive, chatting to it, reproving it, giving it the occasional pat on the back. Leela had become convinced that the TARDIS *was* alive. She treated it like a minor god, to be flattered and cajoled. She would have garlanded the console with flowers and offered the occasional sacrifice if the Doctor had let her. What worried Leela at the moment was the fact that the centre column of the console had stopped moving up and down, which meant that the TARDIS had stopped.

Had the Doctor, mysteriously absent in some other part of the ship, ordered the TARDIS to stop? Had it decided to stop of its own accord? Or had it broken down in some way?

At Leela's feet there was a kind of robot dog, with squared-off body and head, antennae for ears and tail. It was called K9.

K9 looked like a dog, and sometimes even acted like one, but in reality he was a complex and sophisticated computer, built by a space-travelling scientist who missed the dog he'd left behind on Earth. K9 was self-powered, independently mobile, and had built-in offensive capabilities—in other words, a blaster in his nose.

Leela said, 'K9, we've stopped!'

K9 cocked his metal head in a curiously dog-like fashion. 'Affirmative!'

'We've stopped dead!'

'Negative dead.' Like all computers, K9 had a very literal mind.

The Doctor marched into the control room. He was wearing a painter's smock, a floppy beret, and carrying an enormous brush.

'What on Earth have you been doing, Doctor?'

'Decorating,' said the Doctor with dignity.

'I thought the TARDIS could maintain itself?'

'Well, so she can, after a fashion. Can't always trust her taste though. You remember I didn't like the way she did the spare control room, all that white?'

Leela nodded.

'Well, when I told her, she said I was welcome to try and do better myself. So I am!' The Doctor flourished his paintbrush, sending drips of blue paint everywhere. 'Rather a pleasing shade of aquamarine, don't you think?'

'Doctor, we've stopped. Nothing's gone wrong, has it?'

The Doctor wandered over to the console. 'Not so far, no.'

'Then why are we not going anywhere?'

The Doctor touched a control and a wall-panel slid back to reveal a monitor screen. It was blank. The Doctor frowned and checked the controls again. 'That's intensely interesting! Do you realise, Leela, we've stopped because there's nowhere to go? As far as I can make out, we're on the edge of the cosmos, the very frontiers of creation, the boundary between *is* and *isn't*. Or isn't yet, anyway. Don't you think that's interesting?'

'Well, I suppose so ...'

'What?' The Doctor peered into the blackness on the screen. 'I feel just like a goldfish, looking out into a new world!'

'But it's just black nothing out there. We're stuck here on our own, and there's just—nothing!'

From somewhere near ground level there came an electronic voice. 'We are not alone!'

The Doctor stared at Leela in indignation. 'Nothing? What do you mean, nothing?'

'Nothing!' said Leela defiantly.

'But it's a magnificent nothingness! Do you realise, at any minute, any second, a whole new world could be born out there, and we'd be the first—'

K9 piped up again. 'We are not the first!'

The Doctor ignored him. '—the first intelligent—' he glanced at Leela, 'well, semi-intelligent beings to witness the spectacle.'

'We are not alone!'

'What does he mean, not alone?' demanded the Doctor irritably.

'I don't know!'

K9 was happy to explain. 'We are not the first. We are not alone!' He glided closer. 'Receptors indicate pulsing. Pulsing characteristic of ion drive system. The inference would be: spacecraft in vicinity.'

'Where?'

K9 reeled off a string of spatial co-ordinates. 'Thirty-four, seven, zero, one, seventeen, fifty, zero, five ...'

The Doctor hurried to the console. 'Beyond visual range. Might get it on audio.' He reached for the audio-scanner controls and began tracking them delicately to and fro. Suddenly a faint but regular electronic pulsing came from the speaker. 'Listen, Leela, listen ... Ion drive or I'm a budgie's cousin!'

'Affirmative, ion drive,' said K9 importantly. 'Doctor's family grouping, negative.'

'Oh, shut up, K9!'

'Doctor!' said Leela reproachfully.

'I can tell him to shut up if I want to ...'

Leela glanced at the screen, and suddenly realised it was no longer blank. A fiery point of light had appeared at its centre. It seemed to be getting bigger, and it *was* getting bigger. 'Doctor, look!'

By now the light was a fiery whirlpool, almost filling the monitor screen. The Doctor gave a yell of alarm.

'What is it, Doctor?'

'A spiral nebula! A gas cloud, coalescing to form a whole new star system, sucking in everything around it like a whirlpool ...'

'Including us?'

'If we're not careful.' The Doctor was busy trying to break the TARDIS free of the nebula's pull. 'It's time we got out of here!'

He increased the power, but the nebula sucked the TARDIS closer, closer ... The Doctor's mind was racing. Trying to work out the balance of opposing forces and calculate the best possible escape-path.

Suddenly he realised there was a computer at his feet, able to do the job even quicker. 'K9! Optimum escape trajectory, quickly!'

K9 whirred briefly, and his eye-screens lit up. 'Thirty-four, seven, zero, one, seventeen, fifty, zero, five ...'

Leela found the figures strangely familiar. 'Isn't that where that ... ion drive thing was coming from? Where the space ship is?'

'Yes—but I'll just have to risk it.'

The spiral nebula hung in the blackness of space like a giant flaming catherine wheel, a whirlpool of fire sucking the square blue shape of the TARDIS closer, closer ... The TARDIS disappeared.

Chapter Two

The Minyans

The giant space ship was time-battered, space-weathered, almost a derelict. The big square hull was patched and scarred and worn, like the enormous fin of the solar sail.

Propelled by the faint but steady pulsing of its ion drive, the vessel sped steadily towards a distant spiral nebula, so far away that it was little more than a blazing point of light in the blackness of space.

Inside the space ship, there was an impression of massive, worn-out yet somehow still-functioning machinery. The control room was enormous with ribbed steel walls and great arched metal instrument banks set about the floor. At the front, where the control room narrowed with the nose of the ship, a great curved viewing-port was set into the wall. Below it was the raised command deck, with a semi-circle of padded acceleration couches set around the main control consoles.

Tala was piloting the ship on manual and visual control systems. She was a tall woman, incredibly old, face seamed and wrinkled, hair grey and wispy. Nevertheless, her hands moved over the controls with total confidence. There were three other crew members. On Tala's right in the command chair was Jackson, captain of this strange vessel. A massive figure, square-jawed, with iron-grey hair, he sat gazing at the viewing-port, hands resting on his knees, like some heroic statue.

Next to him was Herrick, younger, round-faced, curly-haired, a man who should have been full of vitality and enthusiasm. Instead he was slumped at his post, as if overcome by weariness.

Orfe, the fourth member of the crew, sat at a sub-control console, to Tala's left. Tall and lean, with a long, quizzical face, Orfe looked like a born joker. But he studied his instruments with the same gloomy intensity as the others.

All four astronauts were strong and fit; all except Tala, relatively young. But all four seemed in the grip of some terrible lassitude, as if every word, every gesture cost tremendous effort. An atmosphere of doom lay over the entire ship. They were rallying themselves to deal with a minor crisis—a mysterious, unexplained noise ...

Tala finished checking the scanners. 'Nothing up front, Captain.' She rubbed her hand over her eyes. 'Only the spiral nebula on two, four, zero.'

'All right, Tala, stay on watch. Orfe, check that nebula.'

'Nebula on two, four, zero, checking,' said Orfe mechanically. 'Couldn't have been the nebula, Captain, it's too far away.'

'Herrick, have you got anything?'

'Nothing on targeter, sir. There's no trace, no blip, nothing.'

Jackson shook his head, as if to clear it. 'All right,

let's think it through again. It's not inside, it's not outside, nobody saw it and we got no trace. But we all heard it—didn't we?' One by one the others nodded. '*Then what was it?* Orfe, re-run the tape, let's hear it again.'

A strange, wheezing, groaning sound filled the control room.

As the noise faded away, Jackson looked round. 'Now then, was that noise generated inside or outside the ship? Has anybody ever heard anything like it before?'

Like lethargic marionettes, the others all shook their heads.

'All right, Orfe, run it through computer ident.'

. 'Ident running, sir.' If the sound, or anything like it, had ever been encountered before, the fact would be recorded in the computer's memory-bank.

With infinite, weary patience, they sat and waited.

The Doctor looked up from the scanner. 'As far as I can gather, we've managed to materialise *inside* something else—a space ship presumably. Probably the one K9 spotted.'

'Affirmative, Master.'

Leela looked at the scanner. It showed metal walls all round. 'What do we do now?'

The Doctor was stripping off his painter's smock and beret and replacing them with his usual hat, coat and immensely long multi-coloured scarf. 'We're well clear of the nebula by now, so we could just go on our way ...'

'But you don't want to?'

'Well, we could just take a quick look round,' suggested the Doctor hopefully. 'I'm rather intrigued to know what a space ship's doing, wandering along the fringes of the Universe.'

Brave as Leela was, she had a strong streak of primitive caution. In Leela's world danger had been all around—the aim was to keep away from it and stay alive. She had never quite understood the Doctor's habit of cheerfully rushing into some unknown peril out of sheer curiosity. 'Will it be safe, going out there?'

'Shouldn't think so for a moment!' The Doctor opened the doors, and led the way outside. Leela followed, K9 glided after them.

They were in a huge gloomy metal chamber, lined with racks holding a variety of strangely shaped devices. Opposite the TARDIS was a massive steel door.

Leela sniffed the atmosphere, like a wild beast entering a strange jungle. 'The air is stale.'

Hands plunged deep into his pockets, the Doctor stood gazing around him. He nodded absently.

Instinctively checking for an escape route, Leela hurried to the door. 'It's locked!' As she took her hands away from the door, her fingers were covered with dust. 'Nobody's been in here for years.'

Carefully the Doctor lifted a round metallic object from a wall-rack and hefted it in his hand.

He studied its design. 'Made in Minyos, made in Minyos,' he muttered. 'Got it! The Minyans of Minyos. This could be a Minyan patrol vessel.' He turned to Leela. 'Have you ever heard of the Flying Dutchman?'

'No.'

'Pity, I've often wanted to know who he was.' The Doctor went down on one knee and held the metal sphere close to K9's nose. 'Dating, K9?'

There was a buzz and a whirr as K9's sensors went into action. 'Isotope decay rate indicates one hundred K range.'

'Yes, I thought as much.'

Leela sighed. 'Oh yes, me too!'

The Doctor fitted the metal sphere carefully back into its rack. 'This fission grenade is a hundred thousand years old,' he said impressively. 'The Minyan civilisation was destroyed a hundred thousand years ago, on the other side of the Universe.'

'Come on, Doctor—explain!' Leela said.

Orfe studied the flow of symbols across the computer read-out screen. 'Ident concluded, sir. Sound identified as relative dimensional stabiliser in materialisation phase. As used in ...' Orfe stopped, unable to believe what he was reading.

'As used in what?'

'As used in the time ships of the gods.'

The Doctor was delivering a potted version of Minyan history. 'It was what happened on Minyos that led the Time Lords to develop the policy of non-intervention.'

'Non-what?'

'Non interfering in other people's business! You see, when we landed on Minyos, the Minyans thought we were gods—which was very flattering, of course. We were new to space exploration, and we thought we could help.'

'What did you do?'

'Oh, we gave them all kinds of medical and scientific aid, better communications, better weapons. Little things like that.'

'What happened?'

'They kicked us out at gunpoint, then went to war with each other. Learned how to split the atom, discovered the toothbrush, and finally split the planet.'

'Then this ship must have got away before the planet was destroyed?'

'That's right.'

'You said that was a hundred thousand years ago. Nobody lives for a hundred thousand years—do they?'

Tala continued piloting the ship on manual. She was dizzy now, great waves of blackness swirling before her eyes. She shook her head to clear it, hunching forward over the controls, her wrinkled face twisting in concentration. She looked older than ever now.

Unaware of Tala's condition, Orfe and Herrick were arguing heatedly. 'If it is the gods,' Orfe was saying patiently, 'they'll help us. They'll help us with the Quest.'

Herrick's voice was shaking with anger. 'Help us? Like they helped us before, I suppose? Helped us to destroy ourselves. If it is the gods—and there's no way we can tell, because that computer's worn out like everything else on this ship—but if it is the gods, then they're the reason for it all.'

Jackson intervened. 'Control yourself, Herrick. The reason for what?'

'Well, everything,' spluttered Herrick furiously. 'The Quest, *everything*! They're playing games with us! They do, you know. The gods use us for their sport. Time Lords! We should have wiped out the lot of them when we had the chance.'

Orfe shook his head. 'We brought our destruction upon ourselves.'

The argument raged on. As the catastrophe had approached, the doomed Minyans had split into two opposing schools of thought. Some thought that the terrible wars devastating the planet were the fault of the Minyans themselves. They had misused the gifts the Time Lords had given them. The second, and far larger party blamed everything on the Time Lords, saying that the crisis would never have occurred if the Minyans had been allowed to develop at their own pace.

Orfe belonged to the first party, Herrick to the second, and they had been through this argument many times before.

Finally Herrick jumped to his feet, reaching for his blaster. 'Pacifist!' he snarled contemptuously. 'Well, I'll tell you this, Orfe, if I get one of your precious Time Lords in my sights, I'll dematerialise him for good! And if they are on board this ship, then I'll soon sniff 'em out!'

Jackson intervened. 'Sit down, Herrick, you're supposed to be on duty.'

'But, sir!'

'*Sit down.*'

Herrick subsided. Jackson glanced at his console. 'Time for the next scan. Tala, set her up for the next sweep.'

'Yes, sir.' Tala's face was turned away from Jackson, and he couldn't see the terrible weariness that filled it. She began setting up the scan, fighting off the waves of dizziness that came ever more frequently now.

Jackson turned to Orfe. 'Next quadrant please, Orfe.'

'Course two, four, zero and cube, sir.'

'Two, four, zero and cube,' repeated Tala. 'It's going to take us very close to that spiral nebula, Captain.'

'I know. But we have no choice. The Quest is the Quest.'

'The Quest is the Quest,' repeated Orfe ritually. It was the answer to all questions, all objections.

Hand on the main power control, Tala suddenly collapsed, jamming the lever fully forward with the weight of her body. Controls locked, the Minyan patrol vessel sped straight for the blazing heart of the spiral nebula.

Chapter Three

The Intruders

The sudden dip and lurch of the space ship sent the Doctor and Leela to the floor in a heap. Even K9 shot forwards, bumping his nose against the metal wall.

The ship steadied and the Doctor picked himself up. 'You all right, K9?'

'Affirmative.'

Leela got to her feet—a little put out that the Doctor seemed more worried about K9 than he was about her. 'What happened?'

'Trouble,' said the Doctor laconically. 'Blast that door open, K9!'

K9 swivelled to face the door, and the muzzle of his blaster protruded from beneath his nose. But nothing happened. Apparently the sudden jolt had affected him after all.

'Blaster malfunction,' said K9. 'Blaster malfunction, blaster malfunction, blaster malfunction ...'

The Doctor bent over him. 'One of the circuits must have jammed.'

Leela strode swiftly over to the nearest wall-rack and selected one of the strangely shaped weapons. It was a kind of giant blaster, with a built-in square shield between butt and nozzle, so that whoever was using it had cover from the weapons of his enemies.

The firing mechanism was unfamiliar, but Leela had a natural instinct for any kind of weapon. She flicked off the safety-catch, trained the shield gun on the doorway and fired.

There was a sudden roar of power and the door disintegrated in a shower of molten metal. Leela flicked back the safety-catch and looked down at the shield gun in awe. 'What is this thing?'

'It's a Lieberman maser,' said the Doctor grimly. 'Fires charged particles along a laser beam. Don't ever play with strange weapons, Leela.'

'No, Doctor,' said Leela obediently. But she tightened her grip on the shield gun. If there was going to be trouble, this was just the kind of weapon she needed.

'And if you must carry it, switch the safety-catch off!'

'Yes, Doctor.' Leela switched off the safety-catch, so that the weapon was ready for firing. The Doctor stepped through the smoking hole that had once been a door, and set off along the corridor beyond. Leela and K9 followed.

The Doctor turned, a finger to his lips. 'Sssh!' he said urgently.

'Sssh!' repeated Leela.

K9 cocked his head. 'Sssh? Query Sssh! Please amplify instruction!'

'Shut up and be quiet, K9,' whispered the Doctor. 'Come on!'

Herrick grabbed the unconscious Tala and carried

her to a couch at the side of the control room. Jackson and Orfe were trying to bring the ship back on course.

'She's levelled out,' said Jackson hopefully.

'There's nothing on rudders, sir. We're jammed on maximum power.'

'Do what you can, Orfe. Can you shut down drive?'

Orfe nodded and soon the throb of the ion-drive faded. 'It still won't reduce her speed, sir. She's already reached maximum velocity.'

Jackson looked up at the big forward viewing-port. It was entirely filled by the glowing spiral nebula. The ship was heading straight towards it at frightening speed. 'What about using reverse thrust?'

'No good, sir. We'd just tear the ship in two.'

Jackson sat very still for a moment. 'Right. Give her all the power you can on port, main and auxiliaries. Shut down all starboard propulsion units.'

'Yes, sir!'

Jackson stared at the fiery circle in the viewing-port. 'Unless we manage to veer off before we hit the gravity field that thing will suck us down like a whirlpool.'

Herrick was still trying to revive the unconscious Tala.

'How is she?'

'Not too good, Captain. She's gone past her regen point. Deliberately, just like the others.'

Jackson sighed. There was a specific optimum point for regeneration, and to go beyond it was a form of attempted suicide. In the long years of the mission, several of his crew had deliberately chosen this way out.

'None of us likes it, Herrick, but the Quest is the

Quest. Do you think you can save her?'

'Anything I can do?'

Herrick and Orfe whirled round. In the doorway stood a tall, strangely dressed man. 'How do you do?'

Jackson stared unbelievingly at him. 'Who are you?'

'I'm the Doctor.'

'How did you get in here?'

'Through the door, of course.'

Herrick lunged forward, reaching for his blaster. 'He's one of them—he's a Time Lord!'

Leela appeared behind the Doctor, shield gun in hand. 'Stop!'

Herrick froze. 'I told you, sir. I told you they were on board!'

Leela was concentrating on Herrick. Her instincts told her he was the most dangerous of the group. She didn't notice Orfe moving quietly over to something that looked like a tripod-mounted spotlight. He swung it to cover her and touched a control ...

There was a beam of light, a soft electronic chime, and immediately Leela felt the most extraordinary sensation flooding over her.

Leela had been trained as a warrior, and the softer side of her nature had been repressed from a very early age. But it was still there, and now she felt the extraordinary upsurge of love and tenderness. She gave Orfe a smile of melting affection. 'Thank you,' she said softly.

Herrick sprang forward and snatched the shield gun from Leela's unresisting hands. He jumped back, bringing the gun up to cover the two intruders. 'Get back, both of you. Back against that wall!'

The Doctor obeyed. Leela followed, still smiling happily.

'I'll wipe 'em out now, shall I, sir? Just one quick blast ...'

'Calmly, Herrick. Wait for the word of command.'

Jackson studied the Doctor thoughtfully. 'You say you want to help us?'

'Certainly, if I can.'

'*Are* you a Time Lord?'

The Doctor hesitated. The Minyans had no reason to love his people. But it would be impossible to conceal the truth for long. How else could they have arrived on board, if not in a TARDIS? 'Yes,' he said slowly. 'I'm a Time Lord.'

Herrick's hands tightened on the shield gun. 'Then why did you lie to us, say you were a doctor? I'm going to deal with you now!'

As he raised the shield gun, Jackson snapped, 'Orfe!'

Orfe swivelled the device, there was a beam of light and a chime—and Herrick stepped back, lowering the gun. 'Thank you, Orfe.' He smiled at the Doctor. 'Sorry, friend.'

'That's all right, old chap.' The Doctor looked down at Tala. 'What happened to her?'

Jackson said, 'She passed the regen point and collapsed. We know what to do.'

'Well if you know what to do, why don't you do it?'

'Herrick, take Tala to regen—now!'

'Yes, sir.' Herrick swung Tala's limp body over his shoulder and carried her away.

The Doctor heard a soft voice at his side. 'Doctor!' Leela was gazing across the control room at Orfe with a smile on her face that could only be described as soppy. 'His name is Orfe, Doctor.'

'Yes, that's right.'

Leela sighed. 'What a beautiful name!'

Jackson snapped, 'Orfe, come and look after her, then get back to your post.'

'Yes, sir.' Orfe came over to Leela, took her by the arm and led her away unresisting.

The Doctor shook his head unbelievingly. 'Well, well, well! So you did develop the pacifier after all?'

'Very few though, and too late. That's one of the prototype models. Takes enormous power, and can only be used in the ship.'

'How long does the effect last?'

'It depends.' Jackson glanced across at Leela who was sitting meekly on one of the side couches, gazing adoringly at Orfe. 'Is she a primitive?'

The Doctor smiled, thinking of Leela when she was her normal self. 'Oh, yes. Very!'

'Well, it could take several hours then.' Jackson led the Doctor towards the command deck. 'You say you're a scientist, a doctor?'

'That's right.'

'Of medicine?'

'Of practically everything,' said the Doctor modestly.

'Crystallocybernetics?'

'My dear chap, one of my particular specialities. What's the problem?'

Jackson nodded towards the blazing nebula that filled the screen. 'That is!' He pointed to the main control console. 'And this—it's jammed, and worn out.'

'How much time have we got?'

'We haven't. We're already in the gravitational field. We could still pull free though, if we had the guidance systems working. That's the problem. I think the terminal cores must have fragmented.'

'Mind if I have a look?'

Jackson lifted off the main inspection hatch, and the Doctor peered thoughtfully inside the console. He glanced curiously up at Jackson, struck by a strange lethargy in the captain's manner. Despite his obvious competence he seemed exhausted, weary to the soul, a man operating on the very edge of his reserves. There was something about the others too ... And the old woman who'd collapsed.

Studying the maze of delicate circuitry the Doctor said, 'Been a long trip, has it?'

Jackson was silent for a moment. Then he began to speak, his voice deep and slow, every syllable produced with enormous effort. 'We've been in mission a hundred thousand years, Doctor. The ship wasn't designed for that ... Neither were we. Each one of us has regenerated over a thousand times. Have you any idea what that means?'

The Doctor had. Regeneration can prolong life to an amazing extent, but it was never intended to be a ticket to immortality. If the body regenerates too often, the essential life-force, the soul itself, begins to weary and fail. In time each new lease of life becomes an intolerable burden, until the exhausted spirit longs for the repose of death.

The crew of this ship must have reached and passed that point long, long ago.

Embarrassed, the Doctor said, 'Well, I've been through regeneration a time or two myself. Not pleasant ...' He bent over the console.

In the regeneration room, Herrick laid Tala gently into what looked like a padded coffin, and lowered a transparent cover over her.

He went to a bank of controls, hesitated, then threw the switch. The body of the old woman in the transparent case twisted and writhed ... and changed.

The regeneration method of the Time Lords was largely a natural one. A combination of genetic coding and long yoga-like training enabled them to trigger the regeneration process themselves at the appropriate time. The process used by the Minyans was machine-aided, swift, brutal and mercilessly efficient.

Face filled with compassion, Herrick watched as the old woman in the regeneration-chamber grew younger, younger ...

When the body in the case was that of a girl of twenty-five, the hum of power died away.

Herrick threw back the lid of the regeneration-case, and helped Tala to rise. Shakily at first, but with increasing strength, she walked across the regeneration-chamber to gaze at her reflection in the polished steel mirror.

As she looked at her smooth unwrinkled skin and dark, shining hair, her face filled with despair. 'Again!' she whispered softly.

Once again, she had been sentenced to life.

The Doctor worked on, dismantling circuitry that had worn fragile with unimaginable years of use.

Above him Jackson's voice droned away. It was as if the Doctor's arrival had unlocked a long-dammed flood of speech. 'None of us wants to go on, Doctor, and yet we must. The Quest is the Quest. By now we are like the ship, degenerating faster than we can regenerate ourselves. Not the body, not the mind, but the spirit itself wears out ... we are a ship of ghosts, going on and on, unable to remember why ...'

The Doctor straightened up, his voice cutting across the poetic image. 'This has had it, I'm afraid.' He held out his hand. In it rested a crystal, once sparkling and beautiful, now dull and clouded, its surface crazed by a thousand hair-line cracks. The Doctor tightened his fingers and the crystal exploded in a puff of dust. 'You've no more core crystals?'

'That was the last.'

Crystallocybernetic guidance systems had many advantages, but once the crystals wore out they could never be repaired, only replaced.

Jackson stared at the roaring nebula, filling the entire viewing-port as the ship raced ever closer. 'It's finished, then, finished at last. The Quest is over!'

Chapter Four

The Quest

'Nonsense,' said the Doctor cheerfully. 'One can always bodge something up.' Though in this case it was going to be difficult, he thought. 'Tell me about this Quest of yours?'

'It's for a missing space ship, Doctor ... our sister ship, the P7E. We get signals from time to time, we track it and lose it, track it and lose it ...'

The Doctor felt the long hopeless years of searching that lay behind the words. 'But surely after all this time ... there won't be any survivors?'

'Probably not.'

'Then why go on?'

Jackson paused. 'The P7E was carrying colonists. The entire future of the Minyan race depends on our finding her.'

'Ah, I see! Does the P7E carry regeneration equipment, too?'

'Yes, Doctor. And the most advanced computer we ever developed. Something far more important, too, at least to us. It carried our future, the future of the entire Minyan race.'

'A Race Bank?'

Jackson pointed to a coffin-shaped crystal case set into the main console. It was empty—but through the transparent lid the Doctor could see two shallow depressions; they might have been made to hold two enormous eggs. 'The place is prepared but the Race Banks are not there,' said Jackson sadly. 'They would give us the chance to establish a new people on a new planet—Minyos II.' Jackson stared at the fast-approaching nebula. 'At least, that was the theory. It's all finished now, of course.'

The Doctor's mind had been busy during Jackson's recital. 'Oh, I don't know,' he said cheerfully. 'Seems a pity to give up now, after all you've been through. Anyway, I've had an idea. There might just be a ghost of a chance, if it's at all compatible . . .'

The Doctor pulled a tool kit from under the console and sorted out two metal connector-clips.

'Compatible? If what's compatible?'

'You'll see! K9! Where are you, boy? Come on, heel, K9!'

Jackson watched in astonishment as the robot dog glided into the control room. 'What is it?'

The Doctor knelt down and patted K9's head. 'He's my second-best friend, aren't you, K9?'

'Affirmative.'

The Doctor plunged his arms inside the control console, wrenched out two lengths of cable, fastened the clips to their ends and attached the clips to K9's ears. 'Now, let's try it out. Can you feel anything, K9?'

'Affirmative. Contact established.'

'Good! From now on, you're in charge. We want to avoid that nebula. It's all yours, K9—you're on!'

K9 began to throb with self-importance. 'On line. In link-up. Rudder control positive. Acceleration positive. All systems ready, stand by for g-loading, all systems positive ...' K9's voice speeded to an unintelligible babble as he took over control of the ship. There was a rising throb of power from the drive systems as the ship banked sharply, and a sudden increase in gravitational pull that pressed them back against the acceleration couches. The ship veered again, righted itself, and the intolerable pressure ceased. The roar of the motors dropped to a steady hum, and in the viewing port the nebula dropped away to starboard and began to recede in the distance.

Orfe said shakily, 'We've made it. We made it, Captain!'

Jackson seemed unable to take in the fact of their escape.

Herrick came into the control room, a newly-regenerated Tala by his side.

Captain Jackson rubbed a hand over his eyes, began acting as if nothing had happened. 'Ah, there you are, Tala. I see you came through regen all right. Don't leave it so late next time. I know you're exhausted but the Quest—'

'Is the Quest,' concluded Tala. 'Yes, Captain, I understand.'

'Right, everybody, back on station, it's time for the next sweep. Tala, take over from Orfe.'

Tala moved to the controls, and began operating the scanner beam.

The Doctor looked at the busy scene in mild astonishment. So ingrained was the routine of the ship, that once the crisis was over, Jackson reverted to it without a second thought.

Jackson was telling Herrick what had happened. Herrick stared suspiciously down at K9. 'It's some kind of trick, Captain, a scheme to seize control of the ship.'

'I don't care what it is—we've got full power on all systems for the first time in I don't know how long.'

'He's a Time Lord,' said Herrick obstinately. 'You know what they're like. They can't be trusted. Suppose he's just setting us up for something else, something worse?'

Jackson ignored him. 'Orfe, boost that scanner beam, let's see what we can do on full power. Tala, course two, four, zero, and cube it. Herrick, get back on tracking.'

The Doctor went across to sit beside Leela, who was still gazing longingly across the control room. 'His name is Orfe, Doctor,' she whispered dreamily. 'What a beautiful name!'

The Doctor frowned. Apparently the pacifier beam had had a massive effect on Leela's relatively defenceless mind, with the unfortunate side-effect of fixing her affections on Orfe.

The Doctor decided he'd had enough of this new Leela. He'd better do something about it before the condition became permanent. He leaned forward and touched a finger to her forehead, sending her into a light hypnotic trance. 'Leela? Leela, listen to me. You're primitive, wild, warlike, aggressive, tempestuous—and bad-tempered, too!'

Leela stared mistily at him. 'I am?'

'Yes! You're a warrior, Leela, from a warrior tribe, courageous, indomitable, implacable—impossible!'

Something clicked inside Leela's brain. She shook

her head, stared wildly at the Doctor—then came to her feet in one smooth flowing motion, the knife in her hand inches from his throat. 'That's far enough! You —stay where you are!'

Feeling he'd overdone things a little, the Doctor said, 'No! No! Put that knife away. It's all right, Leela, you were just pacified.'

Leela glared threateningly round the control room. 'Who did it?' she snarled. 'Who did it? I'll kill him!' Her eyes fell on Herrick. 'It was him, wasn't it?' Before the Doctor could stop her, Leela started for Herrick, knife poised to attack.

Orfe looked up. 'It wasn't him—it was me!'

Leela whirled round. 'You?' As she looked at Orfe's kind, quizzical face, the feelings of affection came back for a moment. Torn between conflicting emotions Leela stood paralysed.

The Doctor came and put an arm around her shoulders. 'It's all right, Leela.'

She pulled away. 'You're laughing at me,' she sobbed. 'You're all laughing at me!'

'No, Leela.'

'I'll smash their stupid grins off their stupid faces!'

Herrick shouted, 'Signal on tracker, two, seven.'

'Boost and ident, Orfe.'

'Boost and ident, sir.'

A series of alternating high- and low-pitched beeps filled the control room.

'That's it!' shouted Jackson exultantly. 'It's the P7E. Keep tracking, Orfe. Lock on to her. What's the bearing?'

'Two, four, zero, sir.'

40

'Steering two, four, zero,' confirmed Tala. 'Thrust on maximum.'

Jackson's face was alight with fanatical enthusiasm. 'This time we've got a chance. Stay on that course. Don't lose her, Tala. Don't lose her now.'

The Doctor did some rapid mental calculations, jumped to his feet, and ran across to Jackson's command chair. 'Captain, listen to me ...'

Jackson waved him aside. 'Not now, Doctor. Tala, don't lose her!'

'Jackson, course two, four, zero takes us right back into the nebula!'

'That's right, Doctor. If that's where the P7E is, that's where we go.'

'That could mean destruction!'

'It means the end of the Quest. If P7E went in there, so can we.'

'But P7E didn't go in there,' shouted the Doctor despairingly. 'She couldn't have! She must have been there from the very beginning. The nebula formed around her.'

'How do you know?'

'It's elementary physics—the still centre of the raging storm. She may be in there, and she may be safe— but if you try to reach her, it'll mean your own destruction.'

'If P7E is in there, then we must find her,' said Jackson calmly. 'That is our purpose—destruction is a chance we take. The Quest is the Quest.'

Jackson was quite serious. The long years of searching had made him totally obsessional. If tracking down the P7E meant deliberate suicide, he would steer his ship to destruction in the calm conviction that he was only doing his duty.

'Jackson, I can't allow that!'

'You can't allow it, Doctor? You have no choice.' Jackson nodded to Herrick, and as the Doctor bent to uncouple K9, Herrick tackled him from behind, a forearm like an iron bar across his windpipe.

'K9, stop!' gasped the Doctor.

Leela drew her knife. 'You! Let the Doctor go.'

Jackson was already covering her with his blaster. 'Don't move!'

There was a moment of tense silence, broken by K9's plaintive voice. 'Query stop. Stop what? Please amplify instruction.'

'Doctor, tell it we're going on,' ordered Jackson.

Herrick's arm tightened.

'We're going on, K9,' croaked the Doctor.

Jackson gave a nod of satisfaction. 'Herrick, strap these two into their couches.'

Herrick released the Doctor, stepped back and drew his blaster. 'Quickly, you two.'

The Doctor and Leela were bustled to a spare acceleration couch on the command deck and strapped into place.

'Right,' snapped Jackson. 'Everyone back to their stations. Tala, don't lose that signal!'

On the vision screen, the nebula grew steadily larger.

The Doctor watched it despairingly. It was ironic, he thought. His efforts to pull the TARDIS free of the nebula had landed him on a space ship with a crew of lunatics heading determinedly towards it.

The Doctor saw a swarm of tiny objects swirling about the fringes of the nebula. 'Jackson, look out! We're heading straight into a meteor swarm.' Almost immediately there was a series of clangs and thumps as meteorites began slamming into the hull. If a really big one hit them ...

'Shields up!' ordered Jackson. Heavy metal shields began sliding across the viewing-port. The ship reeled and shook under the continuous impact of the meteorites. It was like being inside a tin can with someone throwing stones at the outside. Throwing, and hitting ...

'Jackson, this is hopeless,' yelled the Doctor.

Leela leaned forward, shouting above the din. 'What's happening?'

'We're being sucked through the outer meteorite layer. The meteorites are smashing us to pieces.'

'What did you say, Doctor?'

Everything went absolutely quiet.

'They're smashing us to—'

The Doctor broke off, his voice loud in the sudden silence.

'They are?' asked Leela, puzzled.

The Doctor sat quiet, trying to work out what was happening. He could hear the signal from the P7E, fading, fading ...

'Damage report?' asked Jackson calmly.

Tala looked up. 'I think we've lost right and left auxiliaries.'

'And the solar sail, plus all external antennae,' said Orfe.

'Hull's taken a battering,' said Herrick. 'Sealer

pumps are still working though.'

Tala completed the report. 'Main drive positive, on course and holding, all major systems functional.'

'Then we go on. Raise the heat shields, Tala, and take her on manual.

Slowly the metal shields slid back, everyone waiting to see what they would reveal.

There was an astonished silence. Through the viewing-port they saw not the fiery nebula, not even the blackness of space. They saw a wall of rocks.

Chapter Five

Buried Alive

Tala was calling out instrument readings. 'Signal fading, sir. Forward visibility nil. We're losing acceleration.'

'Full boost on both motors.'

A grinding roar of power, as the ship's drive was strained to its limits.

'Full power, sir. But we're still slowing down.'

The steady double beat of the P7E faded still further, and became silent. 'Signal going ... signal gone ...' said Tala. 'Acceleration lost ... we're drifting ... all major systems still functional ...'

Jackson hammered a fist down on his console. *'Then why aren't we moving?'*

'Don't you know?' said the Doctor quietly.

'You do, I suppose?'

'What's your normal hull thickness?'

'Three metres twenty.'

The Doctor raised his voice. 'K9, what's our present hull thickness?'

'Hull thickness seventy metres—increasing.'

'Seventy metres!' repeated Jackson unbelievingly.

'We're being buried alive in the heart of a new-born world.'

'That's impossible!'

'No, it's not impossible, Jackson,' said the Doctor

wearily. 'Simply gravity. Elementary physics, remember? This ship is a large heavy object, surrounded by lumps of smaller, lighter material. Our gravitational pull is stronger than theirs. We attract them, they stick to us. The heavier we get, the faster we grow. It all snowballs. We're being buried, barnacled by meteorites. *We're being turned into a planet!*'

The Minyan patrol ship drifted silently through space. It no longer resembled any kind of space craft. It was a huge floating ball of rock, almost indistinguishable from the meteorites surrounding it.

'Still,' said the Doctor cheerfully, 'if it wasn't for our protective layer of debris, the meteorites would have smashed us to smithereens long ago. Can't have everything, can you?'

'Look at him,' shouted Herrick. 'He's laughing at us!'

'Is there any way out, Doctor?' asked Jackson.

'I don't known ... You could try using the laser cannon.'

'Of course, we'll blast a tunnel and force our way out on ion drive!' Jackson swung round. 'Tala, do we have the power?'

'It would take up all our reserve, Captain. It could blow the drive units.'

'It's either that or be stuck here for eternity.' Jackson came to a decision. 'We'll try it. Herrick, fire both laser cannons full power.'

Herrick gave him a dubious look, and reached for the laser controls. 'Fire one! Fire two!' There was a kind of muffled boom, and the red glare of the laser beams filled the control room.

The rock wall beyond the viewing-ports remained unchanged.

K9's voice cut into the tense silence. 'Hull thickness, ninety metres, increasing ... ninety-five metres, increasing.'

'Carry on firing, Herrick,' said the Doctor calmly.

Herrick looked at Jackson, who hesitated, then nodded. Again there came the roar of the cannon, and the red glare of the laser beams.

The needles on Tala's instruments were quivering in the red danger sector. 'The forward hull's buckling, sir!'

'Carry on, Herrick,' ordered the Doctor.

Herrick fired again.

'Stop it,' screamed Tala. 'We're melting our own hull!'

'Carry on, Herrick,' said the Doctor implacably. 'Keep firing—it's our only chance!'

Herrick fired again and again until the laser controls erupted into sparks and smoke beneath his hands. 'It's no use—the cannons are disintegrating!'

The electronic voice of K9 reported, 'Hull thickness, one hundred metres.' Suddenly it rose to a higher note. 'Penetration—you have penetration!'

'Now, Tala,' shouted Jackson.

Tala thrust the power-controls to maximum. There was a roar of tortured engines as the ship juddered, vibrated and broke free. The wall of meteorites was gone. In its place an enormous grey sphere filled the viewing-port.

Jackson stared at it in astonished fascination. 'What is it, Doctor?'

'That's your P7E.'

'Power reserves exhausted, Captain,' reported Tala.

Jackson didn't seem to hear her. 'What do you mean, Doctor, the P7E? That's a planet!'

'It's where your signal was coming from, all the same.'

'Where?'

'Right in the middle of it. The planet must have actually formed around it.'

Tala raised her voice. 'Captain, the power's gone.'

'That's it then,' said Jackson dully. 'There's nothing else we can do.'

Leela watched the grey planet zoom closer, filling the entire viewing-port. 'Are we going to crash?'

The Doctor nodded. 'At full speed. Sit down, everyone!'

Obediently the crew returned to their acceleration couches and strapped themselves in.

They waited in tense silence. In a calm electronic voice K9 began counting off the seconds to their doom. 'Impact in eleven seconds. Ten, nine, eight, seven, six, five, four, three, two, one . . .'

The Minyan space ship sped through the thin atmosphere surrounding the planet, and headed for the level grey surface like a dart hurled at the ground. It struck the surface of the planet at maximum speed—and disappeared silently beneath it.

The Doctor opened his eyes. 'It's all right, Leela, you can look now.'

Leela opened her eyes and looked around, wondering why she was still alive.

The Doctor raised his voice. 'Relax, everyone. We've hit a soft planet, one still in process of formation. With any luck only the planetary core will be really solid—and this stuff should slow us down so we don't hit it with much of a bang.'

'We are two hundred and fifty kilometres below planetary surface,' reported K9. 'Speed decreasing.'

The danger over, Jackson's one obsessive interest came to life again. 'Orfe, the signal. See if you can find the signal.'

Orfe adjusted a control and the strange double beat filled the control room again, louder and clearer than before. 'That's it,' he shouted. 'Contact!'

'We've found it,' breathed Jackson. 'The P7E at last!'

The Doctor looked at Leela. 'Fascinating, isn't it? The Quest and nothing but the Quest!'

Orfe was using the communicator. 'Minyan Patrol Vessel to P7E ... Minyan Patrol Vessel to P7E ...'

There was no reply. 'They must hear us,' muttered Jackson. 'We're right on top of them!'

There was a jarring crash, and everything went black.

Chapter Six

The Trogs

The crashed space ship was jammed into the heart of the planet like a dart hurled into an ant-heap.

The network of interlinked tunnels which honeycombed the planetary core had been destroyed at the point of impact, and there were cracks and subsidences and roof-falls in the area all around. Like terrified ants, swarms of scrawny, under-sized, ragged men and women ran to and fro through the tunnels, screaming with fear.

'The sky! The sky is falling.'

'It's all coming down on us ...'

'Run ... run ...'

To these people, the network of branching tunnels *was* the world, its roof the sky. Here they were born, here they toiled away their short, miserable lives, and here they died, to be replaced by others of the same kind.

Even so, they had their dreams, their legends. Stories that life had not always been like this, prophecies that one day they would escape, through the sky, to the stars—whatever they were.

But such talk was forbidden, to be discussed only in whispers in the crowded darkness of the sleeping-caves. Meanwhile they toiled and died, obeying the

Guards, who were ruled by the Seers, who were servants of the Oracle. Rebels were dealt with swiftly and mercilessly—the Sword of Sacrifice awaited anyone who questioned the established order.

There had been a particularly severe rock-fall in one of the main tunnels, not far from the crash area. A whole section of roof had come down, obliterating an entire family who had been working together, as was the custom. Now they were all buried beneath the rock-pile, the wife and the two daughters. There were two survivors, father and son, who had been chipping at the rock a little apart from the others.

The father was called Idmon, a wizened, balding man, dressed in the brief, ragged smock that all the tunnel workers wore. His son, Idas, was still wiry and strong, though in a very few years he would become a replica of his father. Men aged fast in the tunnels.

The two men were scrabbling frantically, hopelessly at the rock-pile that had buried their loved ones, choking in the powered rock-dust that filled the air. They were sobbing as they worked, the tears making little streaks in their grime-covered faces. A huddled group of their fellow-workers stood watching them apathetically.

Idmon straightened up from his hopeless task, and turned on the watchers. 'Help us, damn you—help us!'

'They won't help, father,' said Idas wearily. 'Don't waste your breath!'

Life in the tunnels didn't encourage the nobler qualities. The struggle to survive took up all your strength—there was none to spare for helping others.

The watchers turned away, ignoring the old man's appeal.

Idmon shook his skinny fist at them. 'Then may the sky fall on you! May the sky fall on your families!'

'Father, no,' shouted Idas. 'The Guards will hear!' Any reference to Skyfalls, actual or possible, was strictly forbidden.

Idmon was beside himself with rage and grief. 'May the sky fall on your loved ones, as it has on mine!' he screamed.

'Please, father, just dig!'

Idmon began scrabbling frantically at the rockpile. 'My children,' he sobbed. 'My children ...'

High in the tunnel wall, a remote control camera studied the scene with its single crystal eye.

In a steel-walled control room, the camera's eye view was reproduced on a monitor screen, one of a bank that filled most of one wall.

Two sinister black-clad figures entered the room. They wore pointed hoods, eyes gleaming evilly through the slits. Their appearance was deliberately designed to be terrifying. They were Senior Guards, and their task was to maintain order in the tunnels. They pulled off their hoods, revealing heavy brutal faces.

The spy-cameras were one of the Guards' most important weapons. Anything that happened in the tunnels could be seen and heard in this central control room. If necessary, a squad of Guards was despatched to deal with any emergency.

The wall to the left of the monitor bank bore a huge electronic chart of the tunnel system. It looked like an enormous tree, with the great main tunnel the trunk, smaller ones branches and twigs. The chart was constantly being altered as new tunnels were built, and old ones closed down. So vast was the network that it was impossible to monitor it all at once. The Guards maintained a kind of random scan, hoping that any trouble would reveal itself sooner or later. The Guard began punching up random shots of the tunnels.

This particular Guard was called Tarn; his colleague's name was Rask. Both were big, powerful men, very different from the wizened tunnel workers. They regarded the 'Trogs', as they called them, as little better than animals, necessary evils to be kept constantly under control. Trogs didn't use the regeneration process to prolong their lives. They were weak and ignorant and ragged, creatures to be despised.

It never occurred to Tarn or Rask or any of the other Guards that generations of ill-treatment had made the Trogs what they were. Guards took it for granted that the Trogs obeyed them—just as they themselves obeyed the Seers, and the Seers obeyed the Oracle, who ruled over all.

Tarn looked up from the monitor. 'Skyfall on Eight —and a Trog making trouble.'

Rask was studying the wall chart. Sections of the design were flickering to designate damaged tunnels. Others were dark, where tunnels had been closed down. He turned and glanced at the monitor. 'Many dead?'

'Not enough,' said Tarn brutally. 'There were two

more births yesterday, they breed like animals. What we need is a good sacrifice. Trogs always work better after a sacrifice!'

Rask put on his hood. 'Maybe you're right. I'll take out a patrol and pick up that troublemaker.'

A few minutes later he was leading a squad of hooded figures through the tunnels.

Inside the crashed patrol vessel, things were getting back to normal. The dim emergency lights were on, and everyone had picked themselves up, none the worse except for a collection of bruises. The Doctor and Leela had been released, their prisoner status forgotten. Now they were all gathered expectantly in the short corridor to the airlock, the Minyans in surface patrol suits.

'Everything's ready, sir,' reported Orfe.

'Right. Open up.'

The airlock door slid open—to reveal a wall of solid rock.

The Doctor examined it. 'Igneus haematite by the look of it—we must have reached the core of the planet.'

Leela struggled to remember her recently acquired scientific education. 'I thought you told me planets had fire in the middle.'

'Did I? Well, old planets like Earth maybe, but new ones like this sometimes have a molten slurry around a solid core. We're on the very edge of creation here, Leela, a place of cosmic experiment. All the laws of science may be in a state of flux!'

Leela sighed. As usual, the Doctor's explanation left her no wiser.

The Doctor prodded the rock wall. 'All we need to do now is burrow our way out of here.'

'How, Doctor?' asked Jackson helplessly. 'The ship's power system is self-regenerating—it will re-charge itself from the radiation of the planet. But that will take time. At the moment we've no power, no energy-source at all.'

'Oh, I don't know about that,' said the Doctor cheerfully. 'What about the shield guns?'

Jackson frowned, annoyed that he hadn't thought of this himself. The shield guns had an almost inexhaustible atomic power pack in the butt. 'Yes, of course. Herrick, get the shield guns, right away!'

The rock pile was so huge it would have taken days to clear it away. By now anyone underneath it was certainly dead. Idmon had realised the hopelessness of his task and had given up. Crazed with grief and rage, he was again haranguing the little group around him, ignoring the terrified Idas's attempts to shut him up.

'You all know we're slaves to the Guards," he shouted. 'The Guards are slaves to the Seers, the Seers to the Oracle. We're *all* slaves. But we know the answer, don't we? We all know the answer because it was prophesied long ago. Escape!' He pointed upwards. 'Escape to the stars!'

A harsh voice shouted, 'Now!' and hooded figures sprang from the shadows. Idmon's audience screamed and fled in terror, while Idmon himself was seized and borne to the ground.

Idas moved to help him, but Idmon screamed, 'No, Idas—run!'

Idas turned and fled.

'After him!' screamed Rask.

Idas scrambled up the rock pile, two Guards close behind him. There was a tiny gap at the top, and Idas wriggled through with ease. It took the bulkier Guards some time to follow, and by the time they were through the gap, Idas was disappearing round a bend in the tunnel. They set off after him.

Rask jabbed Idmon in the ribs with a booted foot. 'Heresy, treason, incitement to escape. Quite a list.'

Idmon glared defiantly at the hooded figure above him.

'My son's a fugitive, my wife and daughters are dead. What more can you do to me now?'

Rask kicked him again. 'On your feet, Trog. You know the penalty for your crimes. The Sword of Sacrifice awaits you.'

Idas fled through the tunnels, a hooded figure close behind him. He had managed to lose one Guard, but the other was fitter, more persistent, and more cunning. Nothing Idas could do seemed to shake him off.

Idas ran on, gasping for breath, determined not to surrender. Better a quick death by blaster bolt than the long-drawn-out ordeal of the Sacrifice.

He came to an open space where two tunnels met,

and sprinted desperately for cover.

The Guard raised his blaster. 'Stop, Trog, or I'll fire.'

Idas ran on. The Guard fired and a green flash lit up the gloom of the tunnel. Idas screamed and fell, rolling over and over, clutching his right leg. He slammed against the wall and lay still.

The Guard moved towards him.

Suddenly Idas sprang to his feet, and staggered into the nearest tunnel at a limping run.

Before the astonished Guard could fire again, he had disappeared into the darkness.

The Guard used the communicator in the butt of his blaster. 'Suspect sighted on Eight, moving into Nine. In pursuit.'

He moved off purposefully down the tunnel after Idas. The Trog was wounded now, and that would slow him down.

He was as good as dead.

Chapter Seven

Skyfall on Nine

The Doctor and Herrick were wrangling over the shield gun.

'No, no, no,' said the Doctor. 'Hold it like this, and aim there—that's the weak point.'

Herrick looked at Jackson, who nodded wearily. 'Better do as he says.'

Herrick raised the gun and fired, and the centre of the rock-wall melted away. He peered cautiously through the ragged hole. 'We're through to the other side, Captain. Looks like a cavern or a tunnel or something.'

He set off through the gap, and Jackson followed. They clambered through to the other side, and looked around. They were in a long gloomy tunnel carved from reddishly glowing rock, stretching away into the distance on either side. Dim working lights gleamed at intervals in the walls, and here and there oddly shaped crystalline outcrops reflected their glow.

Close to where they were standing, and in several other places, the tunnel was partly blocked by huge chunks of rubble where sections of the roof seemed to have caved in.

Herrick ran his hand along the tunnel wall. 'None

of this lot's natural, sir. It's all been hacked out of solid rock.'

'Hacked out by whom, or what, I wonder?' Jackson looked up at the ceiling, and saw something metallic sliding down a rail set high in the wall. 'Get down, Herrick!'

They crouched behind the rubble, and the device glided smoothly by, disappearing into the gloom.

'It's all right, sir,' whispered Herrick. 'It's moving on. Do you think it was looking for us?'

'It was looking for someone,' said Jackson grimly. 'Well, at least we know the planet's inhabited. We'd better go back in the ship.'

The others were still waiting in the airlock-corridor and there was a babble of questions.

Jackson said, 'We've found tunnel workings and a surveillance system, so we know that whatever life there is here is intelligent. We must be on guard.'

'Oh, get on with it, Jackson,' said the Doctor impatiently.

The other crew members gave him reproving looks as Jackson went on. 'Our objective is to locate the P7E and remove the Race Bank cylinders to a place of safety. The Quest is the Quest.'

'The Quest is the Quest,' chanted the crew dutifully.

'Herrick, issue the shield guns. Orfe, Tala, silent routine.'

Herrick went out first, and Jackson ushered the others through the airlock. When the Doctor and Leela reached the door, Jackson said, 'No, Doctor, not you.'

'The Quest is the Quest!' said the Doctor hopefully.

'Our Quest, Doctor, not yours.'

The Doctor stepped back. 'You're quite right,' he said meekly, and closed the airlock door behind Jackson.

Leela tugged at his sleeve. 'Doctor, this is our chance.'

'What chance?'

'They've all gone. Why don't we just unplug K9, get back in the TARDIS and go on our way?'

In some ways it was the obvious course, realised the Doctor, and he hadn't considered it for a moment. 'What, and leave all these people in the lurch?'

'We don't owe them anything. Let them look after themselves.'

'Go away never knowing how things turned out? I'm surprised at you, Leela. Don't you want to know what happened to the P7E?'

Leela sighed in resignation as the Doctor opened the airlock door, and led the way through the gap.

They emerged into the tunnel and stood looking about them. 'Welcome to the Underworld,' said the Doctor. His voice echoed eerily through the darkness.

Leela shivered. It was dark and gloomy, the air was musty and the tunnel seemed to stretch away for ever. She could just see the Minyan crew in the distance. 'I suppose we're going to follow them?'

'Of course.'

'What about K9?'

'Oh, he'll be all right. He's building up his strength, regenerating his energy-banks, like the ship itself.'

'How? There's no power source here.'

The Doctor tapped the wall. 'Oh yes there is. Radiation!'

'Radiation? That's lucky, isn't it, Doctor?'

'Of course it isn't! Igneous rock core, new planet, bound to be radiation. Luck! Physics isn't luck, Leela. Physics is fact.' The Doctor paused, considering. 'Or should that be physics *are* fact? Is fact, are fact, never mind! Why do you think these tunnels were dug out?'

'I don't know.'

'Energy! We're in a kind of giant mine. Whoever inhabits this planet uses the rock for fuel. Food, too, I shouldn't wonder. You can't survive on a new planet with a soul full of hope and fresh air, you know. Did I ever tell you about the time I went to Aberdeen?' he went on chattily.

'What? Oh yes, the Granite City.'

'That's right. Do you know, the people of Aberdeen absorb more radiation from the granite than people who work every day in nuclear power plants?'

'Is that good?'

'Well, of course it is! It proves that organisms can adapt to all sorts of environments, even ones like this with a high radiation content.'

Leela heard the patter of footsteps coming towards them. 'Look out,' she whispered, and pulled the Doctor into shelter behind some rubble.

A thin ragged figure appeared out of the darkness, and shot past them at a limping run, disappearing into the gap that led to the airlock.

'He moved like a wounded animal,' whispered Leela.

'Why was he so frightened?'

'Let's go and ask him.' The Doctor started to rise, but Leela pulled him down.

'No, wait. The hunters are coming.'

A group of sinister-looking hooded figures ran out of the darkness.

Their leader looked round. 'He can't be far. Check those fallen rocks, over by that gap.'

The Doctor could see, though as yet the Guards could not, that the hunted man was crouched panting just inside the gap. The Guards would see him soon, and he was too exhausted to run. And if they found the fugitive, they would find the ship ...

He tapped Leela on the shoulder, stood up, and gave a piercing whistle. The Guards swung round. The Doctor and Leela pelted off down the tunnels, leading the hunters away from their quarry.

'Aliens! After them!' screamed the leader. The Guards tore down the tunnel.

Idas got painfully to his feet and clambered through the gap. Before him was a kind of steel door. He pushed it open, clambered through, staggered a few paces and collapsed, exhausted. The Doctor and Leela ran on. It wasn't long before the pursuing Guards began to overhaul them. They were strong, fit men for all their size, and they were far more accustomed to the tunnels than the two they were chasing.

The Doctor and Leela rounded a bend in the tunnel and found themselves in a kind of loading bay. A recess in the wall held a line of simple dump-trucks, and tracks led away into the darkness of a side tunnel.

The Doctor held up the heavy plastic sheeting over

a half-empty truck and motioned to Leela. 'Quick, get inside.'

Leela scrambled into the truck and the Doctor climbed in after her, pulling the plastic sheet to cover them. They crouched down, waiting.

A sharp bit of rock dug into the Doctor's knee and he shifted position. 'Keep still,' hissed Leela fiercely. She was completely motionless, like a hunted animal in a thicket.

They heard footsteps come closer, closer and then stop. There was a murmur of voices—their hunters had stopped for a conference.

'Oh, for a force-weapon,' breathed Leela. 'If we had one of those shield guns ...'

'Ssh! Listen!' whispered the Doctor.

One voice, obviously that of the squad leader, cut through a babble of discussion. 'Well, they're not here, are they? Must have dodged us and doubled back. These damn Trogs know the tunnels like the back of their hands.'

'I'm not so sure they were Trogs,' objected another voice. 'Did you see the size of them, and the way they were dressed?'

'Well, whatever they were, there are ways of dealing with them.' The voice changed its tone. 'Security? Rask here. We're getting nowhere, not enough men. We're clearing out. I want Nine closed down, main and ancillary workings. Stand by for fumigation, as soon as we're clear.' The voice changed again. 'All right, let's get moving—unless you want to be fumigated!'

The footsteps moved away. A minute or two later,

the Doctor scrambled out of the truck. 'Fumigation?
I don't like the sound of that. They're going to smoke
us out like badgers. Come on, Leela, we'd better get
back into the ship. We left the door open!'

They began moving back the way they had come,
keeping a wary eye out for Guards. They reached the
main tunnel, and the gap in the wall without incident.
Soon they were going through the airlock and back
into the ship.

Suddenly Leela pointed downwards. 'Look, Doctor,
blood!' A scattered line of dots led down the corridor.

Leela drew her knife, and began following the trail.
She turned the corner, caught sight of a crouching
figure and sprang, bearing her opponent to the floor.
They struggled, but Leela soon realised her opponent
was putting up only the feeblest resistance. Pinning
him down with one hand she held her knife to his
throat. 'Surrender or die!'

'No ... no ...' croaked a feeble voice.

The Doctor came running up. 'Get off him, Leela,
you're terrifying the poor fellow!'

'I am?' Leela released her victim and got up. He
didn't seem much of a foe when you got a good look at
him. A skinny, undersized youth dressed in tattered
rags, with an ugly wound in his right thigh.

'He's wounded, poor chap,' said the Doctor gently.
'He is the one we saw running away.'

Their captive was still crouched quivering on the
floor, evidently expecting immediate execution. The
Doctor put a hand on his thin shoulders and gently
eased him to a sitting position against the wall. 'It's
all right, old chap, we're your friends.'

The man looked wonderingly at the Doctor, then cowered back at the sight of Leela standing over him, knife in hand.

The Doctor said, 'She won't hurt you. She's a friend, too. Her name is Leela.'

'She is strong and fierce,' muttered the man. 'Like the Guards.'

The Doctor was examining the wound on the man's leg.

'It is bad?' asked Leela.

'Bad enough. Fetch me the medikit from the command deck, will you, Leela? White box with a red circle on it, in a wall bracket behind the main control console.'

Leela hurried off muttering, 'White box with red circle. White box with red circle.'

The Doctor sat on his heels next to the wounded man. 'What's your name?'

'Idas.'

'Hello, Idas. I'm the Doctor. Are you frightened?' Idas nodded silently.

'Don't be,' said the Doctor gently. 'I told you—we're friends.'

Meanwhile the Minyan party had been marching steadily along the seemingly endless tunnel. They rounded a bend and found themselves at a junction point where the tunnel divided.

The party came to a halt. 'These tunnels could stretch on for miles,' said Jackson wearily. 'The P7E must be at the end of one of them—but which?'

'We could split up, sir,' suggested Orfe. 'Form two parties, take one tunnel each.'

'Too dangerous. What if we run into trouble? We're few enough as it is.' Jackson thought for a moment. Herrick was the boldest and most resourceful of the little party, though his natural truculence might lead him into trouble. 'Herrick, go and scout down the left-hand tunnel. Look out for any signs of life. If you find anything promising, come back and let us know. If you run into trouble, come back even quicker. And don't get lost!'

Herrick grinned confidently, pleased to be chosen for the mission. 'Don't worry, sir, I've got the markers.' He took an adhesive metal disc from a belt pouch and slapped it on the rocks where the tunnel divided. Shield gun held before him, he moved warily down the tunnel.

Jackson turned to the others. 'Tala, Orfe, you'd better get some rest. Break out the emergency rations.'

All three produced food-concentrate tablets from their belts and found seats on the rubble. They sat resting, looking round uneasily, waiting for Herrick to return.

Herrick marched down the tunnel with his usual cheerful confidence. Before very long, he came to another junction. He stuck on a marker, chose left at random, and went on. He found another junction and yet another. This whole area seemed honeycombed. Herrick decided the inhabitants of this strange underworld must have been mining, following some particular mineral seam as it twisted and turned through the rock. He made yet another left turn and found he was looking at one of his own markers. He had been going round in a circle.

He turned to retrace his steps—and found himself facing a hooded figure with a blaster.

A harsh voice ordered, 'Stop, Trog, or I'll fire!'

Herrick kept moving. 'Who the blazes are you?'

'Stop, Trog!'

'Don't you Trog me,' said Herrick indignantly. He took another step forward.

The hooded figure raised its weapon and fired.

Chapter Eight

The Smoke

Herrick brought up his own weapon at the same moment, but not to fire it. He simply held the shield gun in front of him. The Guard's own maser beam was reflected straight back on him, killing him instantly.

Herrick gave a grunt of satisfaction, moved forward and picked up the man's gun, examining it curiously. To his astonishment a tinny voice came from the butt.

'Guard Klimt! Guard Klimt! Clear Tunnel Nine Complex, clear Tunnel Nine Complex. It is being closed for fumigation. Guard Klimt, come in please!'

Herrick found the communicator button and pressed it. 'Guard Klimt has just retired—suddenly!'

There was a pause and the astonished voice said, 'Who is that? Identify yourself.'

'This is Trog Herrick here! Who are you?'

In the security area Tarn looked up at Rask, who had just returned from his unsuccessful hunt for Idas. 'He says he's a Trog—and he's armed. Close down Complex Nine for fumigation—now!'

Rask moved to a nearby console and began operating controls. 'Complex Nine closing down.'

Tarn watched him, worried. Armed, organised revolt by the Trogs was the one thing he and his kind had always feared. So far it had never happened. There had only been the occasional solitary rebel, like Idmon, now a prisoner awaiting sacrifice.

Fumigation was one of the Guards' main weapons in keeping the Trogs under control. Any of the tunnels could be closed off by steel shutters and flooded with gas from a series of vents in the walls. The ostensible purpose was to keep the tunnels free of disease. In reality, fumigation was a way of reminding any potential troublemakers that their lives were in the hands of the Guards.

Tarn remembered the cheerful, arrogant voice that had come over the communicator. 'That was no Trog! A Trog wouldn't dare attack a Guard and take his gun—and as for being insolent over the communicator ...'

Rask stared thoughtfully at the winking lights on the electronic map. 'Well, the two I saw in the tunnels were no Trogs.'

'Aliens?'

'We still don't know what caused that Skyfall.'

Tarn came to join him at the map. Light-bars were appearing across Tunnel Nine, showing that the steel shutters were sliding into place. Tarn smiled. 'Well, we'll know soon, won't we—when we find the bodies.'

Herrick was hurrying down the side tunnels, following his markers to find his way back to the others. To his vast relief he saw them in the distance standing at the junction to the main tunnel. 'Captain!'

Jackson peered down the tunnel. 'Herrick? Are you all right? I thought I heard a blaster.'

Herrick began running towards him. 'Yes, I'm fine, I—'

A steel shutter slammed across the tunnel in front of him.

'Nine close-down completed,' reported Rask.

Tarn studied the map for a moment. 'Fumigate the whole of Complex Nine.'

'It's a big area,' warned Rask. 'The gas will take quite some time to build up to effective levels.'

'That doesn't matter. We're in no hurry—are we?'

Rask's hand reached for a main control lever. 'Very well,' he said formally. 'Fumigating—now!'

Jackson gave the shutter an angry kick, and stepped back. 'Herrick, stand clear,' he yelled. He turned to Tala and Orfe. 'All right, blast it!'

They raised their shield guns and the shutter disappeared in an explosion of smoke and flame. A few moments later, Herrick appeared.

'Did you find it?' shouted Jackson. 'Did you find the P7E?'

'No, sir. It's just a sort of maze in there—all I found was some kind of Guard. He tried to kill me with this!' Herrick held out the dead Guard's weapon.

'Who was he?'

'No idea, sir. There's a communicator built into that thing. It called him Guard Klimt.'

Jackson took the gun and examined it. 'Minyan design. Must have been looted from the P7E.'

'What do we do now, sir?' asked Tala.

'Go on with the Quest, of course.'

As they moved off down the other branch of the tunnel, Orfe paused. 'I thought I heard something, sir. A kind of hissing ...'

Tala pointed. 'Look, Captain!'

Swirls of vapour were drifting down the tunnel towards them.

Leela was looking on while the Doctor cleaned the wound on Idas's leg. 'That's better. It shouldn't take long now.'

'Are you a Seer?'

'A what? No, I'm the Doctor. Soon be finished, old chap.' The Doctor rummaged in the medikit and produced a couple of aerosol sprays. He used the first to sterilise the wound, and the second to spray a fine layer of plasti-skin over the area. 'Leela, just go and unplug K9 for me, will you?'

'I've just been all the way up to the command deck for your medikit box.'

'Linked up like that, K9's supervising the working of the whole ship.' Suddenly the lights returned to their normal brightness. The Doctor looked up. 'You see? The ship's recharging its energy-banks. It can look after itself now. Tell K9 to concentrate on his own re-charging, I shall need him soon.'

'All right, Doctor, I'll go and unplug K9,' said Leela. She hurried away.

The Doctor sprayed a final layer of plasti-skin on Idas's wound. Idas winced. 'Stings, does it?' said the Doctor cheerfully. 'That's good, shows it's working!'

Idas straightened his leg. There was very little sign of the wound by now, and it had almost stopped hurting. 'Are you a Seer?' he asked again.

'No, Idas, just a traveller.'

'Where from? Where do you come from?'

'From the sky!'

'You lie!' said Idas fiercely. 'There is nothing but chaos above the sky.'

'Oh, very well then, from the stars.'

Idas stared at him in awe. 'My father talked about the stars. There is an old prophecy among the slaves, handed on for generations. It says that one day gods will come from the stars to set us free. Are you a god?'

The Doctor smiled wryly, remembering his people's intervention on Minyos. 'No, Idas,' he said gently. 'I'm not a god. But I'd still like to help you if I can. Could you take me to your father?'

Sadly, Idas shook his head. 'It is not possible.'

'Why not?'

'When the Skyfall happened, all my family were buried. My father became crazed and spoke against the Guards, so they took him away.'

'What will happen to him?'

'They will sacrifice him to the Oracle. There is nothing anyone can do.' There was the resignation of generations of slavery in Idas's voice.

'Oh, isn't there?' said the Doctor indignantly. 'We'll see about that! Try to stand up.'

Idas got to his feet, and found to his astonishment that his leg would bear his weight without hurting.

Leela came hurrying along the corridor. 'I have unplugged K9, Doctor. He says his re-charging is almost complete.'

'Splendid! This is Idas, Leela.'

'Hullo, Idas,' said Leela. Idas shrank away, still not convinced she wasn't dangerous.

'They're going to sacrifice his father,' explained the Doctor.

'Look, Doctor!' shouted Leela.

The Doctor and Idas turned. A cloud of white vapour was drifting down the corridor towards them.

'It is the Smoke,' screamed Idas. 'You have brought me into a trap to kill me.' He lunged at the Doctor's throat and they fell together into the cloud.

Leela jumped into the gas after them, trying to pull the Doctor free. There was a brief flurry of arms and legs, and after a moment the Doctor surfaced, dragging an unconscious Idas after him. Leela followed. Coughing and choking they retreated down the corridor.

The Doctor shoved Idas towards Leela. 'Get him to the command deck, you'll be all right there for a while.' He began wrapping the folds of his scarf over his mouth and nose.

Leela stared at him. 'Where are you going, Doctor?'

'Outside to try to do something about this gas.'

'You'll suffocate out there! Can't you just keep it out of the ship? If we close the airlock door ...'

'I could try—but what about all the others? They're out in those tunnels somewhere, you know. Just get Idas to the command deck.'

Pulling his scarf up below his eyes, the Doctor dashed through the wall of smoke towards the airlock.

Jackson and the others were plodding doggedly along a smoke-filled tunnel, blasting the steel doors as they came to them. They had their helmet-visors down and there was an air supply in their back-packs. But the supply was limited and already it was dangerously low.

If they didn't find a way out of the smoke soon, they would have to open their helmets—and the smoke would choke them.

Protected only by his scarf, the Doctor felt his way along the walls of the tunnel. His eyes were streaming, and he was beginning to cough.

The Doctor's respiratory system was far more efficient than that of any human being, but he needed oxygen to survive as much as anyone else.

The gas wasn't poisonous as such; it was some kind of fumigant smoke. But if it built up sufficiently, it would asphyxiate him all the same.

At last he found what he was looking for—an inspection hatch beside a smoke-pouring grille. Smoke doesn't just move of its own accord. It has to be pumped—which meant that somewhere there had to be a pumping station.

The Doctor produced his sonic screwdriver, undid the hatch fastening and lifted it off. He surveyed the tangle of circuitry with satisfaction. 'Whatever blows can be made to suck,' he thought grimly. 'If I disconnect this here, reverse the polarity, and re-connect here ...'

Fanning the smoke away with his hat, the Doctor set to work. It was an intricate job, and it wasn't made any easier by the fact that his head was beginning to swim. The circuit panels started blurring before his eyes.

Doggedly the Doctor worked on, while the smoke in the tunnel built up into a dense, impenetrable wall.

He was making the final cross-connection when the sonic screwdriver slipped from his fingers and he collapsed unconscious.

Smoke from the vent swirled round his head, in a thick grey cloud.

Chapter Nine

The Mouth of the Dragon

As the Doctor lay unconscious, something strange happened.

Smoke stopped coming out of the vent, and began rushing *into* it, faster and faster like water draining from a tank. All over the Tunnel Nine area the same thing was happening. The smoke began to clear with astonishing speed ...

In the Security section, Tarn was bowing deferentially before his communicator console, acknowledging the instructions of the brown-hooded figure on the screen. 'I obey immediately, Master.' There was both fear and reverence in his voice. He turned to Rask. 'We are ordered to round up the slaves to attend the coming sacrifice.' He broke off in horror. White smoke was pouring from all the ventilators, filling the room ...

Tarn gave a yell of fear. 'The gas—it's getting in! Shut down the fumigation system.'

Coughing and choking, Rask staggered to the console.

The Doctor opened his eyes and saw a wisp of gas drifting past his eyes and into the vent. He smiled. Evidently he *had* finished the job before passing out. He got to his feet, and watched as the last few wisps of gas were whisked away. 'I wonder where it all went?' said the Doctor thoughtfully, and went back to the ship.

When he came on to the command deck, Idas, now recovered, was sitting bolt upright on an acceleration couch, obviously not daring to move. He was staring all round him with wide, astonished eyes.

Leela appeared from the corridor to the armoury, proudly holding another shield gun. 'I have found a weapon, Doctor!'

The Doctor stood staring into nothingness, lost in thought. 'Have you?' he said vaguely.

'Well, we've got to protect ourselves somehow, haven't we?'

Idas looked up as Leela came towards him. 'Are you really from the stars?'

'Yes,' said Leela matter-of-factly.

'The stars,' breathed Idas in wonder. 'They really exist then?'

'Of course they do!'

Idas pointed to the metal ceiling above them. 'And that is not the sky?'

'That is the roof,' said Leela pityingly.

'Roof,' said Idas thoughtfully. 'Will you take me with you when you return to the stars?'

'No,' said Leela.

'Yes,' said the Doctor. 'Or rather the owners of this ship will—I hope! Unfortunately they've got problems.' He looked down at K9 who was peacefully recharging himself. 'Can't lend them you for ever, old chap, can I?'

'Negative, Master.'

'Why do you call this your ship?' asked Idas.

'That's what it is,' said Leela.

Idas shook his head. 'No, no, it is a Citadel. We have a Citadel, too.'

'You do?' said the Doctor with sudden interest. 'Where is it?'

'In the heart of our world. It is where the Guards and the Seers live, in metal rooms like these.' Fear filled Idas's voice. 'We are taken there when they hold the sacrifices. My father will be there now, waiting ...'

The Doctor stared at the guidance-system console, thinking of the shattered crystal. The P7E and this one were sister ships. Besides, he didn't approve of human sacrifice. 'Can you take us to this Citadel of yours?'

'I could ... but there is no time now,' said Idas mournfully.

'No time! Don't ever say that to me, I'm a Time Lord!'

Leela pulled Idas to his feet. 'Do not worry,' she said consolingly. 'The Doctor has saved many fathers. Come.'

Deep within the heart of the planet was another control room, very similar to the one the Doctor had just left. Once it had been the command deck of the P7E, though it was many thousands of years since it

78

had fulfilled that function. Now it was a kind of temple, the computer consoles and control panels draped with rich hangings, smoky temple lamps creating an atmosphere of sinister gloom.

In a sub-control room adjoining the main command deck, Idmon, the father of Idas, lay strapped to a metal trolley, a gag in his mouth. A hooded figure stood watching him from the doorway. It was dressed not in the universal black of the guards but in a garment of sombre brown, ornamented with golden studs. This was Ankh, a Seer, one of the two supreme rulers under the Oracle. Fiery red eyes glinted behind the slits of his hood.

Flanking him stood Tarn and Rask. Ankh spoke in his metallic, inhuman voice. 'Assemble the slaves to witness the sacrifice. They must be reminded who rules here. See that they learn the lesson, Tarn, or you will be next!'

Tarn bowed low. 'Yes, Master. All shall be as you command.'

Ankh turned away. Rask crossed to the trolley and glared down at Idmon. 'Make the most of these few moments, slave. They will be your last!'

Idmon could not move because he was fastened to the trolley, and he could not speak because he was gagged. But as he looked up at Rask, his eyes blazed with defiance.

The Doctor, Leela and Idas moved along the tunnels, K9 trundling along behind them.

The Doctor was questioning Idas about the social

organisation of the planet. 'So the Oracle lives in the Citadel, and tells the two Seers what to do. The Seers tell the Guards, and the Guards tell you?'

Idas nodded.

Leela had been listening to the conversation. 'And you do all the work?'

Idas said sadly, 'Yes. That is how it has always been.'

'Has no one ever thought of revolution?'

'My father did—and now he waits for sacrifice.'

They came to a central junction point, with tunnels branching off on all sides. Idas hesitated, confused. 'There are so many tunnels. It is hard to be sure.'

The Doctor had a thought. 'K9, could you make us a map of this tunnel system?'

'Affirmative, Master.' K9's antennae extended and his eyes lit up. He spun round in a complete circle, as if he were chasing his own tail. Then he stayed, remained completely still for a moment, whirring and clicking busily.

'What's happening?' asked Leela.

'Sssh!' said the Doctor reprovingly. 'He's concentrating!'

'Ready, Master.'

The Doctor stooped and drew a roll of paper from K9's mouth. He held it up. 'Very good, K9. Thank you. Now, I think you'd better go and find Jackson and the others. Bring them back here and then follow on after us, clear?'

'Find, retrieve and follow. Affirmative, Master!' K9 spun round and glided away.

The Doctor held up the map. 'Now then, Idas, K9

has kindly made this for us. Do you recognise it?'

Idas bowed his head in reverence. 'It is the Tree. The Tree of Life.' The complex map with all its main and subsidiary tunnels did look rather like a kind of tree.

'The Tree at the End of the World,' said the Doctor softly. Idas, where are we?'

Idas studied the map for a moment, then pointed. 'Here,' he said confidently.

'Good. And where is the Citadel where they're keeping your father?'

Idas pointed to a squarish shape at the centre of the map.

'I see,' said the Doctor thoughtfully. 'Now, how can we get from where we are to the Citadel—quickly?'

Idas hesitated. 'There is a way—but it is forbidden.'

'Why?'

'It is guarded by invisible dragons. Not even the Guards are allowed to use it. Only the Seers—and they have special powers.'

The Doctor chuckled. 'So do I, Idas. So do I. Anyway, the Tree at the End of the World is always guarded by dragons. Fire dragons with tongues of flame!'

Idas shuddered.

'Do not worry,' said Leela. 'The Doctor has killed dragons before!'

Jackson and his crew were resting at yet another junction. They felt weary and defeated. The mysterious disappearance of the smoke had removed one danger, but after endless searching they still hadn't managed to locate the P7E.

Herrick leaped to his feet, raising his shield gun. 'Something's coming—following us along the tunnel.'

They waited tensely. A squat metallic shape rounded the tunnel and came gliding towards them.

'It's that robot dog of the Doctor's,' said Jackson, amazed. 'What's it doing here?'

K9 glided to a halt. 'I bring instructions from the Doctor,' he said importantly. 'You will accompany me at once, please!'

'Why should we go with you?' demanded Herrick angrily. 'We've got to find the P7E.'

'I have already located the P7E. The Doctor is on the way there now. Please follow me.'

K9 wheeled and set off back down the tunnel. The Minyan crew looked at each other, and then followed obediently. There didn't seem anything else to do.

Idas led the Doctor and Leela down a short dead-end tunnel. It ended in a wall of rock in which were set two massive metal doors.

The Doctor took a step forward. Idas pulled him back. 'No, Doctor, that's where the dragons live.'

'It is, is it? Let's see if they're at home.' The Doctor took an apple from his pocket and handed it to Leela, who took a bite out of it.

'Don't eat it,' ordered the Doctor. 'Throw it!'

Leela tossed the apple towards the door. A lattice-work of lightning flickered across the tunnel, reducing the apple to charred fragments.

The Doctor produced another apple. 'Look for the source-point this time, Leela. The mouth of the dragon.' He tossed the apple, the lightning flickered again, and this time Leela saw the side nozzles projecting the maser-rays.

'Got it, Doctor.'

'Right, give them a blast!'

Leela raised her shield gun and blasted the nozzles, first one side and then the other, turning them into lumps of shapeless metal.

'Now the door!'

A long blast from the shield gun melted the door into nothingness, revealing a square chasm, rather like a lift-shaft.

'In you go,' said the Doctor cheerfully.

Leela went cautiously up to the edge. It was like a lift-shaft all right—but where was the lift? All she could see was a dizzying drop, stretching down and down. 'Oh, no, Doctor, there's nothing there!'

'Oh yes there is. There's gravity.'

Leela looked suspiciously at him. 'Didn't you once tell me gravity makes things fall?'

'That's right—towards the centre. But this is a new-born planet, Leela, on the very edge of creation. Things are different here. We're almost at the centre of the planet. Inside this shaft there will be zero gravity, just as in space. That's my theory, anyway.'

'But it's just a theory?'

'That's right,' said the Doctor cheerfully. 'So I'd better test it!'

He stepped over the edge of the shaft—and stood

suspended in nothingness.

Leela turned to Idas. 'Come on,' she said with resignation, and dragged him bodily into the shaft.

All three hung suspended in space.

'How do we move?' asked Leela.

The Doctor grinned. 'Just push!'

'Push?'

The Doctor nodded. He stretched out until he could reach the side of the shaft, pushed upwards and immediately began drifting down. His voice floated up to them. 'Push!'

Leela turned to Idas. 'Push!' she said fiercely.

Now all three were floating down together.

'You all right, Idas?' called the Doctor.

Idas nodded, paralysed with fear.

They drifted down, down, down ... It was a pleasant enough sensation, decided Leela. But what happened when they reached the bottom?

Absorbed in the new sensation, none of them noticed a spy camera set into the wall of the shaft.

On his monitor screen, Tarn watched the three figures drifting down past the camera's field of vision. Just as he'd suspected—aliens. Two aliens, and a traitor Trog.

He leaned forward to the communications mike. 'Gate patrol—alert! We are being attacked by alien invaders. Prepare an ambush.'

Tarn sat back, well satisfied. When the invaders reached the gates of the Citadel, they would die.

Chapter Ten

The Sword of Sacrifice

In the temple which had once been a space ship, every-thing was ready.

A crowd of ragged slave workers huddled at the back of the huge room, flanked by armed Guards.

There was a murmur of awe as Lakh, the Seer, strode into the temple and bowed low before the screen of flickering light that was the visible manifesta-tion of the Oracle—the god whose presence pervaded the entire temple, the one who had ruled since time began.

Ankh came and ranged himself beside his fellow Seer, bowing low.

The Oracle spoke, its voice a throaty whisper filled with infinite age and wisdom. 'Is the time right?'

Lakh bowed again. 'The time is right.'

'Is the slave ready?'

'The slave is ready.'

'And those who watch?'

'They are filled with fear.'

The questions were part of the time-hallowed ritual of sacrifice.

The dreadful voice whispered, 'Let the sword ask its question.'

'It shall be done!'

Black-hooded Guards pushed forward the trolley to which Idmon was fastened, positioning it in the exact centre of the temple.

Idmon stared upwards, knowing what he would see. Suspended above him was an enormous sword, its needle-sharp point poised above his heart.

The sword was suspended by a silken cord, and the cord ran through two ring bolts in the ceiling. Suspended a little below the tautly-stretched cord was a ceremonial oil-lamp with a tiny naked flame.

It only remained to wait.

In time the cord would char and fray in the rising heat. When the cord snapped, the sword would fall, and Idmon would die.

But not for some time yet. The lamp was some way below the cord, and its flame was turned low. The longer the wait, the greater the opportunity for the victim—and the audience—to reflect on the folly and wickedness of rebellion.

Idmon stared up at the gleaming sword-point and thought about his son, wondering if the boy had got away.

Lakh turned towards the watching slaves, raised his hands and began the ritual.

'Lamp burn, sword fall.

Ask the question that hangs over all.'

The crowd took up the chant. 'Ask the question that hangs over all.'

'... Eventually the flame burns through the rope, and

the sword falls,' said Idas. His face twisted in grief, as he thought of his father.

They were still drifting down the shaft, though the bottom was now in sight.

'It is a very complicated way to kill,' said Leela. 'Why go to so much trouble?'

'Terror,' said the Doctor simply. 'Intimidation! The more ritual and mumbo-jumbo, the greater the effect. That's the whole point of official punishment, eh? Anyway, you can talk, Leela. What about the Test of the Horda?'

Leela nodded. There had been an equally complicated and gruesome ritual on her own planet—though there, at least, the victim did have a chance. The Doctor himself had survived the Test, cutting a thin rope with his cross-bow bolt in time to save himself from dropping into the pit of savage Horda.

She was just about to point this out, when she hit the bottom of the shaft with a gentle bump.

They had arrived.

Jackson, Orfe, Herrick and Tala were running along the corridor that led to the top of the shaft.

They paused when they saw the yawning chasm, but K9 sailed straight on, shooting over the edge of the shaft to hang suspended in space. 'Follow, please,' he piped. 'Faster. Imperative move faster!'

The Doctor, Leela and Idas came out of another short tunnel, and found themselves facing a wide chasm, stretching right across their path.

It was spanned by a narrow metal bridge—and on the other side of the bridge was the P7E.

They could see only one side of the space ship, which appeared to be embedded in solid rock. The bridge led straight to its airlock, which stood invitingly open.

The Doctor strode confidently on to the bridge. More hesitantly, Leela and Idas followed.

They were half-way across when black-hooded Guards appeared in the airlock, covering them with blasters.

They turned. More Guards had taken up positions at the other end of the bridge.

One stood a little apart from the Guards in the airlock, obviously their leader. 'Do not move!' he called. 'You with the weapon, throw it down.'

'Throw it down, Leela,' said the Doctor resignedly. Leela tossed the weapon over the bridge and it spun down and down till it disappeared from sight.

'Move forward,' ordered the commander. 'Bring them inside.' They shuffled forward until they reached the airlock, where hooded Guards surrounded them.

The commander pulled off his hood. Idas shrank back. 'Rask!'

Rask nodded, peering into his face. 'Idas, is it not? You're just in time to follow your father. But first you shall see him die. Bring them to the temple!'

The cord was beginning to burn through. Strand after strand had separated, and now only a few thin threads supported the weight of the sword.

There was a stir as the three prisoners were thrust into the room. Ankh said angrily, 'What is the meaning of this interruption, Rask?'

'I have captured the aliens, Master, and the traitor, Idas!'

Puzzled, Ankh looked to his senior for guidance. Lakh waved his hand, and a Guard with a long pole moved the lamp away from beneath the cord, holding it to one side.

'Bring them forward,' ordered Ankh.

The captives were thrust forward. Lakh studied them. 'Aliens and traitors! They too will answer the Question of the Sword. Let the ceremony continue!'

The Guard released the lamp, allowing it to fall back into place. The cord was very thin now—any moment the last few strands would be snapped by the weight of the sword. They began to unravel ...

'No!' screamed Idas. With one frantic leap, he sprang from the group of prisoners and shoved at Idmon's trolley—just as the sword flashed down. It missed Idmon's body by inches, glanced off the edge of the trolley and clattered to the floor.

There was a gasp of horror at this sacrilege. For a moment no one moved—except the Doctor. He whirled round, knocked down the nearest Guard, snatched the man's blaster and tossed it to Leela. 'Out!' he roared. 'Everybody outside! If any of you want to be free—come with us!'

'Kill them!' screamed Ankh. 'Kill them all!'

A Guard raised his blaster; Leela promptly shot him down.

There was instant pandemonium, terrified slaves milling about the temple in their rush to get clear of the blaster fire. A few of the bolder ones ran forward to follow the Doctor. He snatched up the sword, cut Idmon free of the trolley and pulled him to his feet.

He thrust him towards Leela, who began bustling everyone towards the door. 'Move! Come on, move!' she shouted. 'Come with us, and fight for your freedom!'

'Get them all into the tunnels, Idas,' shouted the Doctor. 'We'll never beat them here!'

The air was full of shouts, screams and the whine of blasters. There was so much noise and confusion now, with slaves running in all directions, that the Guards had to aim their fire carefully for fear of hitting each other or, worse still, of damaging some part of the Oracle.

The Doctor and Leela had no such problem. Leela fired her blaster, the Doctor waved his sword menacingly. Guards and slaves alike gave way before them. In a tightly-packed group, the Doctor and Leela and Idas and Idmon thrust their way towards the door, followed by a few rebel slaves.

'Kill them!' screamed Ankh again. 'Kill them— kill them all!'

Rask, more practically, was speaking into his communicator. 'Gate patrol! There's a breakout. Rebel slaves. Stop them!'

Jackson and his crew followed K9 out of the anti-grav shaft, along the corridor—and found themselves facing the P7E for which they had been searching so long.

For a moment they gazed in awed silence. Then they heard the sounds of screaming and the sizzle of blaster fire coming from the ship.

'There's a battle!' yelled Herrick joyfully, and ran for the bridge.

The Doctor's little group ran down the corridor to the airlock—straight into the advancing gate patrol. Leela drove them back with a barrage of blaster-fire, then swung round and aimed more blasts at the pursuing Guards. 'They've got us on both sides, Doctor,' she shouted.

'We could try rushing them,' suggested Idas. 'We must do something!'

'Hmm,' said the Doctor thoughtfully. He was sure there must be a solution, but for the moment he couldn't seem to think of it.

Suddenly they heard the distinctive roar of a shield gun. Herrick shot down the corridor, and opened fire on the gate patrol. The Guards swung round to deal with the new attacker—and Leela blasted them again.

Now it was the gate patrol who were caught in a crossfire, and they broke and scattered.

Led by Leela and Herrick, the Doctor's party dashed down the corridor and into the airlock. Leela and Herrick stood back to let them through, and then defended their rear with covering fire. Step by step, they fell back until they were on the bridge—all except Herrick, who stayed in position, covering the entrance to the airlock, protecting their retreat.

When everyone was across the bridge, Jackson shouted, 'Herrick! They're all across—come on!'

Herrick was filled with the joy of battle, the kind of berserk bloodlust that made the old Vikings fight till they died beneath a heap of their foes. A Guard edged too far forward in the airlock, and Herrick picked him off. Without looking round he yelled, 'I've waited a long time for this, and I'm not missing it now. Go back, Captain. Goodbye and good luck!'

'Herrick, I order you—' shouted Jackson.

Herrick wasn't listening. Crouched down on one knee so as to get maximum cover from his shield gun, he was methodically raking the airlock with blaster fire. Jackson hesitated. Then with a yell of, 'Goodbye, Herrick!' he ran after the others.

Herrick went on fighting till he was over-run. A dozen Guards rushed him from the airlock doorway, urged on from behind by a furious Rask. The first half-dozen died beneath his fire but the rest leaped over the bodies of their fellows and bore him to the ground. The butt of a blaster thudded against his head.

When the survivors sorted themselves out, Herrick lay like a Viking warrior, surrounded by a ring of dead enemies.

Rask came out of the airlock, and stood looking down at Herrick's body. He jabbed it in the ribs with his boot, and Herrick moaned and stirred.

Rask smiled. 'Good. Not dead—yet! Bring him inside—for questioning!'

Chapter Eleven

The Crusher

In a disused side tunnel, an old hiding place where slaves met for hopeless talk of rebellion, the Doctor and his party were pausing to rest and plan. They had already exchanged stories with Jackson and his crew.

A small group of rebellious slaves had followed them from the P7E. The Doctor was dressing the wounds of their new allies with supplies from the medikits the Minyans carried in their belts. Leela was helping him. The slaves had suffered most in the battle. They had no means of defending themselves, and the Guards had not hesitated to fire whenever they got a clear shot at the crowd.

Leela sprayed a layer of plasti-skin on to the arm of a slave girl called Naia. 'And life has always been like this for your people?'

'We are born, live and die in the tunnels,' said Naia simply. 'There was nothing else—until now. Nothing but the Quota.'

'The Quota?'

Naia picked up a fragment of rock, then threw it to the ground. '*This!* Every day we must carve out so much rock for the Crusher to feed into the Citadel.'

'Why do they need rock?'

'For energy, for fuel, for reprocessing into food. So

we can go on working, to get more rock—unless our lives are ended by a Skyfall.' She laughed bitterly. 'Oh, they say they're accidents, but they're not, not all of them. They use them to keep our numbers down. Just enough of us survive to do the work.'

At the end of the tunnel, Idas was staring longingly at Jackson's shield gun. 'If only we had more of these ...'

Jackson shrugged. 'Even if we had, we can't use the shaft again. They'd be ready for us. They'd wipe us out before we got over the bridge. Is there any other route into the ship?'

Idas shook his head despairingly. 'None that I know of ...'

Leela moved over to the Doctor. 'Doctor, Naia here says they eat rock!'

The Doctor nodded. 'On a new planet like this, who knows what's possible? There could well be nutrients in the rock, and if they were processed properly ...' He grinned. 'Did I ever tell you about the time I went to Blackpool? Everyone eats rock there!'

'Doctor, be serious.'

The Doctor was thinking aloud. 'If they process rock, they must take it into the ship somewhere, mustn't they?'

'Through the Crusher,' said Leela. 'That's what Naia said, anyway.'

'Through the Crusher and into the ship.' The Doctor looked up. 'There is another way in, there has to be!'

Suddenly he changed the subject, following a random thought. 'Why do you think Idas calls the tunnel system the Tree of Life, Leela?'

'Why shouldn't he? No, wait a minute ... Idas has never seen a tree, has he? So why would he call it one?'

'The Tree of Life,' said the Doctor. 'The Race Bank! The gift of immortality, on the Tree of Life ... guarded by the dragon!'

'Surely, Doctor, all this is just a myth, an old story?'

'Ah, but old myths have a grain of truth in them—if you know where to look. Do you know, Leela, everyone here except us comes from the same racial stock as Jackson and his crew?'

'The same stock?'

'How do you think they got here, in the middle of a planet? Seers, Guards, Trogs—they're all descendants of the people who came here on the P7E. Jackson is probably Idas's great-great-great-great-great-grandfather a few thousand times over!'

'Great-great-great—' said Leela, puzzled.

The Doctor grinned. 'Don't worry about it.' He went over to Jackson. 'There *is* another way into the P7E, you know.'

'The bridge will be guarded ...'

'Ah, but what about the other side of the ship—the goods entrance, eh? They still need food, don't they, and they still need fuel, and the rock has to go in somewhere.'

The Doctor beamed. 'Come on, everyone, let's get moving. You lead the way, Idas. Oh, and bring the sword. I've had an idea ...'

Before they realised what was happening the Doctor was bustling them off.

Some time later, after a long and wearying journey through the tunnels, they stood hiding in the entrance to an open area criss-crossed with tracks and filled with dump-trucks. They were watching a gang of weary slaves shove a rock-filled dump-truck along a single-line track.

The track ran up to a rock wall and disappeared into a gaping mouth, from behind which came the sinister grinding sound of the Crusher.

The slaves wheeled the truck to the opening and tipped the load of rocks through the hole. They pushed the empty truck away. Nearby more slaves were waiting to wheel up more rock-filled trucks. From a command-post, black-hooded Guards stood supervising the operation. It all looked like a miniature railway yard, with the sweating bodies of slaves replacing the engines.

The Doctor tapped Jackson on the shoulder. 'There you are! What did I tell you? There's our goods entrance.'

Jackson looked dubious. 'We'll have to overpower the Guards silently, before they can use their weapons. One shot and the alarms will go and they'll know we're inside. It'll be difficult ...'

'But not impossible,' whispered Leela cheerfully, reaching for her knife. This kind of commando operation was just what she liked. 'If we can just get behind them ...'

'Well, it's just about feasible,' admitted Jackson reluctantly. 'If this plan of the Doctor's works.'

'Well, it's not really my plan,' said the Doctor modestly. 'I got it off a chap called Ulysses. He pulled it off a while ago ... Come on!'

He began creeping towards a siding filled with empty trucks.

Herrick recovered consciousness. He tried to move and found himself clamped into a heavy metal chair. A helmet had been fitted over his head. Leads from the helmet ran to a nearby console, where a black-hooded figure stood waiting.

Two more hooded figures dressed in sombre brown were standing over him. Their eyes glinted redly through the eye-slits of their hoods.

'Who the blazes are you?' whispered Herrick weakly.

'We are Seers, servants of the Oracle. I am Ankh, and this is my colleague, Lakh. Where are you from?'

'Minyos.'

A searing pain shot through Herrick's entire body.

'Liar,' said Lakh coldly. 'Minyos was destroyed a hundred thousand years ago.'

Ankh repeated the question. 'Where are you from?'

'Minyos!'

'Liar!' screamed Ankh. More pain. The pain stopped. The man at the console called, 'The readings show that he speaks the truth, Master.'

'Silence,' screamed Ankh. 'We are the only survivors of Minyos.'

'You?' jeered Herrick. 'Never!'

'What do you seek here?' asked Lakh. 'Why have you come?'

'We seek ... the future ...'

'There is more, Master. He is holding back.'

'More!' ordered Lakh.

Another jolt of pain seared through Herrick's body, making him writhe within his bonds. Ankh leaned over him. '*What else?* We can make the brain boil inside your skull. *What else?*'

'All right, all right,' gasped Herrick. 'No reason you shouldn't know. We are Minyans—and we seek the cylinders containing the Race Bank.'

'Race Bank cylinders?' There was genuine puzzlement in Ankh's voice. 'What cylinders?'

'The cylinders contain the genetic inheritance of the Minyan people. They were placed on board this ship, the P7E.'

'You are mistaken,' said Ankh.

'He is lying,' snarled Lakh.

Herrick writhed under another jolt of pain.

'There is no purpose, Master,' called Tarn. 'He speaks the truth—or what he believes is truth.'

'The Quest,' muttered Herrick. 'The Quest is the Quest!'

Lakh leaned over him until he could see nothing but the sinister hood and the glowing red eyes. 'This is not a ship! Not your P7E. There is no such thing as this Race Bank of which you speak.'

'If you were really Minyans you would know,' said Herrick obstinately.

'The Guards and slaves are all of true Minyan

descent. So are we, though we have evolved far beyond them.'

'Then who are you? What are you?'

'We are the Seers, the servants of the Oracle. Our flesh has been changed by the one we serve. See!'

The two sinister figures swept off their hoods—and Herrick gave a gasp of horror. Their heads were made of polished metal, with two great glowing red crystals for eyes.

The servants of the Oracle were no longer human. The heads they wore had been given them by their Master.

One by one the slaves pushed their trucks up to the mouth of the Crusher. One by one the trucks deposited their rocks and were pushed away. There was a steady crunching roar as the Crusher devoured its food.

The last two slaves on the line were Idmon and Idas. They pushed a truck which seemed curiously light. A length of plastic sheeting had been tossed over the top.

The Doctor and Leela were crouched down inside the truck. They heard the roar of the Crusher coming nearer and nearer ...

'Any minute now, Leela,' whispered the Doctor.

But at this point the Doctor's plan went a little astray.

Idas was supposed to stop the truck *before* he tipped it, giving the Doctor and Leela a chance to climb through the hole and work their way round the Crusher and into the ship.

At the last moment his foot turned on a chunk of rock. He stumbled, inadvertently shoving the truck forward.

To his horror it *tipped*—shooting the Doctor and Leela straight towards the Crusher ...

Chapter Twelve

The Battle

Just as the Doctor's truck reached the feeder-hole, a second truck appeared, pushed up by another group of slaves. As it came level with the squad of Guards it stopped. Jackson and Orfe leaped out, shield guns in hand.

As Orfe dropped down from the truck, a Guard raised his blaster. Tala shot from the side tunnel, and the Guard fell—straight on to an alarm button. The howl of a siren filled the air.

More Guards appeared and opened fire on the rebels. Jackson and Orfe fired from behind the truck. Tala and her armed slaves joined in from the side-lines, and the Guards were caught in a deadly cross-fire.

The howl and whine of blasters filled the air.

The Doctor, meanwhile, was clinging to the edge of the truck by his finger tips, trying desperately not to slide out and through the hole. Below him he caught a glimpse of a pit filled with whirring, grinding, sharp tooth cogs, pulverising the chunks of rock into powder.

The metal of the truck was slippery with fine rock-dust, and the Doctor felt his fingers beginning to slide. Leela was scrambling for a hold just above him ... and if she slipped and fell on to him ...

The Doctor felt hands grasping his feet, taking the

weight from his aching fingers. He slid down carefully, and Idas helped him to his feet.

Leela came down after him, and the Doctor helped her from the truck.

He peered through the mouth of the Crusher. It was a steeply slanted shaft, leading straight into a pit filled with grinding machinery. There was no way through it or round it — not in one piece, anyway!

Abandoning his original plan, the Doctor dodged behind the truck. A fierce three-cornered battle was raging all around him. Orfe and Jackson were hiding behind the nearest trucks, exchanging fire with the Guards. Tala and her freed slaves were shooting from the side-lines.

'Come on, Leela!' shouted the Doctor. Ducking and weaving, they ran across to Jackson. At the sight of the Doctor, K9 zipped out of a side tunnel to join them.

'Right,' said the Doctor briskly. 'We haven't much time, so everybody stay calm. K9, back to the ship, check all systems are in order and prepare for blast off. We may be leaving in a bit of a hurry.'

'Affirmative,' said K9 and glided away.

The Doctor turned to Jackson. 'I'm going to try to find some other route to the Oracle. It'll mean working my way round the ship. Can you and the others manage to hold off the Guards?'

'We can try, Doctor,' said Jackson grimly. He ducked as a maser-bolt whizzed past his head.

'Good! Leela, you're coming with me.'

'I'm staying to fight!'

'You're coming with me! You too, Idas. Have you got that sword?'

Idas paused for a moment to clasp hands with his father.

'Take care, my son,' murmured Idmon.

'You too, father.'

'Right, Jackson,' said the Doctor. 'We'll be off. Can you give us covering fire?'

'Ready when you are, Doctor.'

The Doctor sprinted for the side tunnel at the back of the loading area, Leela and Idas at his heels.

Guards opened fire as soon as they broke cover. Jackson and the others replied with a sustained volley from their shield guns. The Doctor and his two companions reached the tunnel entrance and disappeared from sight.

Inside the loading area the battle raged on. More Guards appeared in answer to the alarm summons, but Jackson and the others fought on undismayed, catching the blaster-bolts of their enemies on their shield guns and using the deadly weapons to terrible effect.

Tala and her little army of freed slaves fought like demons. Every time a Guard fell, another slave snatched his weapon and joined the battle.

Soon Jackson realised that something completely unexpected was happening. They were winning. 'Forward!' he yelled and led a charge that drove the Guards back into the tunnels of the ship.

Rask dived into cover and used his communicator, panic in his voice. 'They're driving us back. There are too many of them. They've armed the slaves—it's a full-scale revolt. They're too strong for us, I need reinforcements ...'

Rask and his fellow Guards had been terrorising slaves for too long. They had lost their taste for real fighting.

In the security section, Tarn, Lakh and Ankh listened in horror to the panic-stricken voice babbling from the speaker.

'Hold them!' ordered Tarn. 'You must hold on.'

Ankh thrust him away from the communicator. 'Rask! I order you to stand and fight. You must protect the Oracle.'

'Master, we cannot hold them back much longer. We must retreat!'

'No excuses! Stand and fight!'

Still strapped in the interrogation chair, Herrick laughed despite his weakness. 'There's no stopping us now. A hundred thousand years of searching ... I smell victory!'

Lakh ignored him, turning to his fellow Seer. 'Let us consider. What is more important—these cylinders, or the safety of the Oracle?'

'The Oracle, of course, but—'

'Then should we not give them what they seek and let them depart?'

'But what they seek does not exist!'

'The Oracle will know. Why should we destroy each other?' He went over to Herrick. 'These cylinders—tell us what they look like. If they are indeed here, you shall have them and take them to your comrades.'

'You will set me free?'

'Yes!'

'There are two of them, made of solid gold, and stamped with the mark of Minyos. They are the length of a man's hand.'

'Good. Tarn, tell Rask what we have decided. He is to arrange a truce.'

Tarn hurried to the communicator.

Deep inside the side-tunnels, the Doctor paused at a junction, getting his bearings. 'This way, I think.'

Leela shook her head. 'No.'

'Why not?'

'There are Guards moving this way.'

'Ah!' The Doctor noticed a grille set into the wall. 'What's behind there, Idas? Does it lead inside the Citadel?'

'I don't know.'

'I think it must. Let's find out, shall we?' The Doctor produced his sonic screwdriver, and set to work on the hatch-bolts.

By the time the squad of Guards came thundering down the tunnel it was empty. They were in too much of a hurry to notice that the hatch cover was slightly ajar.

The Doctor and his companions found themselves inside a narrow ventilation shaft, just big enough to move along if you knelt down. The Doctor wriggled happily into its depths, and the others followed.

Some time later, the Doctor paused and raised his hand. 'If my sense of direction's still working, we ought to be nearly there!' They came to another wall vent and Leela peered through.

'Look, Doctor! We've arrived!'

They looked through the grille. Two hooded figures bowed before a screen of flickering lights.

Lakh bowed low before the Oracle. 'The intruders are defeating us,' he said bluntly. 'They will destroy us, destroy *you*, unless they are given these cylinders.'

There was a long pause. Then the husky whisper of the Oracle said, 'Shall they not be destroyed by that which they so desperately desire?'

'Can it be done?'

'Cannot all things be done—by me?'

The light-panel flashed and flickered, there was a hum of power—and a column rose out of the main console. On it rested two golden cylinders.

Lakh took them, bowed low and left the control room.

'They're giving up without a fight?' whispered Leela.

The Doctor rubbed his chin. 'Yes, it certainly seems like it.'

'Why?'

'That's what's worrying me!' In the Doctor's experience rational acceptance of defeat wasn't a characteristic of dictators. Now that he knew what the Oracle was, it seemed even less likely. 'Let's take a look round, shall we?' He set to work on the grille.

*

Crouched down behind one of the trucks, Jackson said suddenly, 'Orfe, listen. They're not firing back!'

The fierce whistle of blaster fire had diminished. All the shooting was coming from their own side.

Jackson shouted, 'Hold your fire, everybody!'

After the uproar of battle, the silence was deafening.

They heard footsteps coming towards them. Rask appeared, his empty hands spread wide before him.

Jackson stood up.

'Careful,' whispered Orfe, 'it could be a trick.'

'Be ready, then.'

Rask came nearer and halted. 'I have been ordered to speak with you.'

'You wish to surrender?'

'We offer a truce.'

'On what terms?'

'You may take what you came for and depart, leaving us to our own ways. Agree—or your comrade will be executed.'

'What comrade? Herrick is dead!'

'You think so, Captain?'

Rask stepped aside. Herrick was behind him, flanked by Guards. He was bruised and limping and weary, but his face was filled with an almost unearthly joy. He held a golden cylinder in each hand. 'Captain, I've got them! The Quest is over!'

Herrick was sobbing with emotion. 'The Quest is over, Captain. *The Quest is over!*'

Jackson walked slowly out to meet him. 'At last,' he whispered. 'At last ...'

*

The Doctor helped Leela and Idas through the grille. 'Stay here!'

Clutching the sword, the Doctor began prowling about the control room. Everything was gloomy and silent. The ceremonial hangings, the temple lamps, the general atmosphere of centuries of disuse gave the place the air of a temple or a tomb.

The Doctor crept stealthily around, studying the disused control console and the unmoving dials. He opened a wall locker and gave a sigh of satisfaction. Shelves lined with spare parts. Burglar-like, the Doctor began filling his pockets.

When he had finished, he closed the locker and walked up to the altar at the end of the control room. He studied the great lamp burning over the light-screen. He bowed and said, 'Hullo, Oracle.'

Lights flickered on the screen, feebly at first and then more vigorously. A husky voice whispered, 'What is it that you want?'

'The cylinders. The Race Bank of the Minyans.'

'Have they not been given?'

'Well—*have* they? That's what I'm asking!'

The voice hissed furiously, 'Who are you to dare question my word?'

'Who do I have to be to dare to question your word? After all, you're only a computer, you know. Programmed to preserve your own safety and that of the ship. You were made to serve, not rule. But after the crash you took over, didn't you? Set up this disgusting society of Guards and Seers and slaves just so *you* could survive!'

'*Who are you?*'

'I'll give you a clue, shall I? If it wasn't for my people you'd never have existed.'

'What people?'

'The ones the Minyans called the gods.'

'Gods!' The husky voice was scornful. 'There are no gods but me! Have I not created myself? Do I not rule? Am I not all-powerful?'

'Well, yes and no ... In here, you are. But nowhere else. You're just another machine with megalomania, another insane object, a self-aggrandising artefact.' The Doctor laughed scornfully and turned away. 'You're nothing—nothing but a mass of superheated junk with delusions of grandeur!'

As the Doctor had hoped, the string of insults provoked the Oracle to uncontrollable rage. 'Nothing!' it roared. 'Am I not the Keeper of the Race Bank of Minyos?'

The Doctor spun round. 'Still the Keeper, are you? So you've still got them!'

'I am the Keeper,' roared the insane voice.

The Doctor was studying the main console. As he'd hoped, there was a socket in its base.

'Keeper? You're nothing but a mechanical money-box—and I've got the key. Give me that sword, Leela.'

Taking the sword from Idas, Leela ran across to the Doctor and passed it over. He thrust it to the hilt into the socket and began turning it like a giant key.

The Oracle gave an agonised shout. 'Destroy him! Destroy! Destroy! Destroy!'

Leela heard the sound of a nearby alarm and the rush of pounding feet. 'Listen, Doctor, the Guards are coming!'

The Doctor ignored her. Once, twice, three times he twisted the sword.

'Leave it, Doctor,' shouted Leela urgently. 'You must come now, or the Guards will kill us.'

'Just one more turn,' gasped the Doctor. 'It's a bit stiff!'

'Destroy! Destroy! Destroy!' boomed the Oracle.

Chapter Thirteen

Doomsday

The Doctor gave one final twist, there was a click—
and a crystal casket bearing two golden cylinders rose
from the console. The Doctor opened it, snatched
them up and thrust them into his pockets. 'No hard
feelings, old chap,' he said, and ran for the grille. Leela
and Idas pulled him through, and they disappeared
into the shaft.

They wriggled through the narrow opening like
rats with a cat after them, and emerged at last into
the tunnel. 'Which way?' gasped Leela.

They could hear the shouts of Guards from somewhere close by.

'We've got to get away from the ship,' said the
Doctor. 'They know this area better than we do.'

Idas said, 'The tunnels, Doctor. Let's go deeper
into the tunnels. I know a place where they'll never
find us. This way!'

Confidently, Idas led them into the maze of tunnels.

In the security section Ankh stood by the surveillance
monitors, watching as Tarn punched up shot after
shot of empty tunnels. Suddenly Tarn caught a
glimpse of three figures disappearing round a corner.
'They have just entered Seven, Master.'

'Good. Close it down and collapse it!'

Tarn moved to a separate control console. All the tunnels had explosive charges set into the roof. It was another method of controlling the Trogs—causing the Skyfalls, the tunnel subsidences that kept down their numbers.

Tarn reached for a control.

Idas led them into a dead-end tunnel. Blocked by a fall of rock, it formed a kind of cave. 'This tunnel is disused—it was blocked by a Skyfall. We should be safe here.'

There was a rumbling crash, and the tunnel entrance collapsed.

Leela jumped back, looking angrily at Idas. 'Safe, you said? Doctor, we're sealed in!'

The Doctor seemed scarcely aware of the catastrophe. He had taken the cylinders from his pockets and was studying them absorbedly.

'Doctor, what's the matter with you?'

The Doctor looked up. 'If these are the Race Bank cylinders—I was just wondering what they've given Jackson!'

Reverently, Jackson placed the two golden cylinders in the casket. 'The Quest is over! Orfe, set course for Minyos II. K9, how do we stand for launch?'

K9 whirred and buzzed. 'Energy absorption still not at optimum level.'

Tala checked the readings. 'There's enough power

to get away, Captain—but only just.'

'I say we go now,' said Herrick explosively. 'We've got what we came for.'

'Negative,' said K9 firmly. 'Personnel incomplete. Doctor and the Mistress not on board.'

Jackson hesitated. The urge to get the Race Bank to Minyos was almost overpowering. But he owed the Doctor a good deal. 'All right, K9, go and find them. Tell them we've got the cylinders and we're leaving *now*!'

'Affirmative!'

The Doctor sat studying the cylinders. Leela felt like shaking him. 'Don't you understand, Doctor? We're trapped! We could be here forever!'

'What? No, no. They'll come and dig us out.'

'Why should they bother?'

'Because we've got something they want,' said the Doctor simply. He hefted the cylinders. 'The Oracle wants these back—remember?'

Tarn was receiving final orders from Lakh. 'At all costs the cylinders must be recovered and replaced. The Oracle commands it. Order a party of slaves to Seven to clear the Skyfall.'

'What of the intruders?'

'When the cylinders are recovered, feed their bodies into the Crusher.'

'It shall be done, Master!'

*

In the control room of the Minyan patrol vessel, everything was ready. Tala, Orfe, and Herrick were already at their posts. Jackson paced to and fro, his eyes on the corridor to the airlock.

'Secondary checks complete,' reported Tala.

'Third and final check commencing,' said Orfe.

Jackson stared at the gleaming cylinders and again at the door. 'Come on, Doctor. *Come on!*'

Leela pointed to the rockfall that had trapped them. 'Look, Doctor! Something's happening.'

They all looked. The rock surface was stirring, smoking. As they stepped back the rocks exploded into a kind of tunnel—through it appeared K9.

The Doctor chuckled. 'There you are, K9! What kept you?'

'Gratitude unnecessary,' said K9 imperturbably. 'Speed vital. Please hurry, Master!'

Jackson made his decision. 'We'll have to leave them. Commence final countdown.'

Orfe began counting. 'Ten ... nine ... eight ...'

'Run up drive.'

'Seven ... six ... five ...'

'Drive running,' reported Tala.

'Four ... three ... two ...'

'Pressurise and prepare for blast off.'

'One ...'

The Doctor shot through the control room door, Leela and Idas close behind him. 'Stop! Jackson, *here* are your Race Banks. The real ones!' He held up the cylinders.

Jackson stared at them, then at the two identical cylinders in the casket. 'Then what are those?'

The Doctor gave him the real cylinders and took the others from the casket. 'That's what I intend to find out. K9, see what you can make of these.' He knelt and held them under the little automaton's nose.

It didn't take K9's scanners long to find the answer. 'Analysis indicates fission grenades, Master.'

The Doctor tried to unscrew one of the cylinders.

'Negative! Do not proceed! Impossible to defuse. Grenades programmed to self-detonate shortly. Explosive content in excess of two thousand megatons. Attempt to defuse will detonate immediately.'

'How long have we got—if I leave them alone?'

'Accurate estimate impossible. Timing mechanism shielded.'

Almost automatically Jackson put the genuine cylinders in their casket. 'What are we going to do, Doctor?'

The Doctor looked at the two camouflaged atom-bombs in his hands. 'I think I'd better get rid of these, don't you?' he said mildly.

'Affirmative,' said K9.

But the Doctor had already left the control room.

'Wait, Doctor,' shouted Leela, and ran after him. Idas hesitated a moment and then followed.

They came out of the ship in time to see the tail of the Doctor's scarf disappearing round the tunnel bend. 'Come on,' said Leela. 'He may need us. After him!'

'*Why* have they not been found?' whispered the Oracle angrily.

Ankh bowed low. 'When the slaves cleared the Sky-fall the intruders had already gone.'

'Shall they not be found?' demanded the Oracle almost petulantly. 'Is that not my purpose?'

It had ruled for so long that it was unable to understand that its will could be crossed, let alone that it could fail.

'They shall be found,' promised Ankh. 'It shall be done as you command. Your servant Rask searches for them now...'

The Doctor shot round a bend and ran straight into Rask and his squad who were herding along a mob of slaves. For a moment they all stared at each other in mutual surprise.

The Doctor said politely, 'Excuse me, could you direct me to the Oracle? I'm a stranger here.'

'I'll take those cylinders, Doctor,' snarled Rask.

'I wouldn't if I were you. They won't do you any—'

'Give them here!' Rask snatched the cylinders from the Doctor's hands. 'Guards, take care of him. Make sure you finish him off—throw him into the Crusher. I shall take the cylinders back to the Citadel.' Rask was eager to grab the credit of success.

'You're making a terrible mistake,' said the Doctor. 'Those aren't what you want at all!'

Rask laughed. 'You can do better than that, Doctor.' He hurried away.

'Ah well,' said the Doctor thoughtfully. He looked

at the Guards. 'Killing me won't solve anything, you know. Those cylinders were bombs.'

The Guards levelled their blasters.

There was a sudden crackle of blaster fire from *behind* him and the Doctor promptly threw himself to the ground. When he looked up the Guards were fleeing or dead, and Leela was running towards him. 'Doctor, are you all right?'

He straightened up. 'Yes, I think so. Let's get out of here, we've not got much time ... Idas, bring your people.'

Idas turned to the cowering slaves. 'Listen to me, all of you. The prophecy has been fulfilled, our gods have come to save us. We can escape to the stars. Skyfall in Tunnel Seven. Bring your families, tell the others. Our gods await us!'

Lakh hurried up to the Oracle with the cylinders. 'They have been found, great one.'

'Replace them, quickly. They must never leave my keeping again.'

Ankh replaced the cylinders in the casket, and it sank slowly out of sight.

There was an astonishing scene outside the airlock of the Minyan patrol vessel. A long line of slaves, men, women, old people, children, was filing through the airlock, bustled along by the Doctor, who was acting as a kind of commissionaire, helped by Leela and Idas. 'Come along now, come along,' shouted the Doctor cheerfully. 'Plenty of room for everyone. Everything's going to be all right. Move along now!'

A furious Jackson pushed his way out through the airlock. 'What's going on here, Doctor? Get these people off my ship. We can't carry all this weight, we're too low on fuel.'

'You'll have to carry them,' said the Doctor grimly. 'This planet's about to explode.'

'Get them off,' insisted Jackson. 'I'm sorry, Doctor, but I must safeguard the Race Banks—for the future of the Minyan people.'

The Doctor gripped his arm. 'Listen, Jackson, these *are* your people. They're descendants of those who came on the P7E.'

'We can't take the weight,' said Jackson desperately.

'You've got to. Your only hope is to go, and go now. Get back to the command deck.'

Jackson hesitated, then turned and forced his way through the crowd.

The Doctor went on chivvying the slaves. 'Come on now, everyone inside. When you get in, just sit down and stay calm!'

They got them all in at last and a furious Herrick slammed and locked the airlock. 'Outer section sealed.'

The Doctor looked round the command deck. There were slaves everywhere, against the walls, across the floor, leaning against the consoles. Most of them were out of sight, stowed away in the holds and the storage areas, but there were still enough left over to overflow into the control room.

Jackson picked his way through the litter of prone bodies to his command chair. 'Run up on drive.'

'Drive running!'

'Prepare to blast off!'

Orfe began counting. 'Ten ... nine ... eight ... seven, six, five, four, three, two, one—blast off!'

Slowly, painfully slowly, the Minyan space ship broke free of the soft planetary surface and launched itself towards the stars. Ankh watched it go on a surface monitor, and looked triumphantly at Lakh. 'They have cleared the surface. Soon they will be blown to dust!'

The frantic clamour of an alarm bell sent him running to the main control room.

The Oracle's lights were flashing in a frenzy of agitation. 'I have analysed the cylinders. *These* are the bombs. Get rid of them or we shall all be destroyed.'

Lakh took the cylinders. 'How—where?' he asked helplessly. 'There is no time.'

'Defuse them—now!'

The space ship rose, rose ... hovered for a moment, and began to fall back towards the grey surface of the planet. The combination of extra weight and low energy-levels made it impossible for the ion-drive to pull the ship free ...

'More power,' shouted Jackson. 'We're falling back!'

Tala looked up despairingly. 'There is no more.'

The Doctor and Leela entered from the hold, where they had been trying to reassure the panic-stricken slaves. 'Everything all right, Jackson?' asked the Doctor cheerfully.

'No, it isn't! We don't have enough power to reach escape velocity. You know why, don't you, Doctor? It's the extra weight!'

'Oh, come on, Jackson, don't despair. Be brave! Why don't you sit down?'

Despairingly Jackson sank into his command chair. On the monitor the planet surface rushed ever closer.

Ankh clawed desperately at the gold sphere. 'It is not possible to defuse this.'

'Why? *Why?*'

'Because you made it so!'

There was a silence. The Oracle whispered wearily, 'I have failed in my duty. I deserve—destruction.'

The cylinder in Ankh's hand began to glow. The glow grew brighter, brighter, till it consumed the control room, the P7E and eventually the planet itself.

The planet exploded into a billion fragments of rocky debris.

The Doctor watched the explosion on the ship's monitor screen. 'There she goes. No planetary gravity to hold you now, Jackson—no planet! Prepare to ride the blast!'

Released from the pull of gravity, the P7E bucketed for a moment in the shock-wave, then streaked out into deep space.

In the control room there was an atmosphere of jubilation.

'We've made it,' shouted Orfe. 'We've made it!'

'Speed?' asked Jackson.

'Four-sevenths light.'

'Course?'

'One, two, zero.'

'How long to Minyos II?'

'Three hundred and seventy years,' said Herrick. He grinned. 'That's nothing, is it, Captain?'

The Doctor was unloading a series of strangely shaped objects on to the top of the console. 'I picked up one or two spare parts for you on the P7E—including a spare set of guidance crystals.' He bent down and patted K9. 'So you won't need my friend here any more.'

The Doctor and Leela began leaving the control room, K9 trundling after them.

'Aren't you coming with us to Minyos II?' asked Jackson, astonished.

Hurriedly the Doctor shook his head. 'Sorry, no time. I'm very busy, you know.' He paused, and smiled. 'Goodbye—Jason!'

'Goodbye, Doctor.'

A chorus of thanks and farewells came from the crew. But the Doctor and his companions had gone.

A few minutes later a strange, wheezing, groaning sound echoed through the ship. Then it died away ...

Chapter Fourteen

The Legend

Magnificent in painter's smock and floppy beret, the Doctor was preparing to get on with his decorating. Leela watched him resignedly. A sudden thought struck her. 'Doctor?'

The Doctor was busily cleaning an enormous brush. 'Um?'

'Why did you call him Jason?'

'Who?'

'Jackson! When you were saying goodbye, you called him Jason.'

The Doctor scratched his head, leaving a streak of white paint in his hair. 'I called Jackson Jason?'

'Yes!' said Leela, exasperated. 'Is Jackson Jason?'

The Doctor put his paintbrush down, and stared into space. 'No, no, no. Jason was another captain. He was on a long Quest, too . . .'

Not surprisingly, the legends of Ancient Greece meant nothing to Leela. 'I don't understand, Doctor.'

'Ah!' The Doctor smiled. 'He was looking for the Golden Fleece.'

'Did he find it?'

'Oh yes, he found it in the end. Hanging on the Tree at the End of the World. You know, Leela, perhaps those old legends aren't so much stories from the past as prophecies of the future ...' Pleased with this rather fanciful idea, the Doctor glanced down. 'What do you say, K9?'

Automatons have no time for imaginative theories. 'Negative!' said K9 firmly.

'Negative?' The Doctor was outraged at this abrupt dismissal of his new theory. He stared at Leela. 'What did he say?'

'He said, negative!'

'Negative?' spluttered the Doctor. 'What does he know, eh? Can he ... can he paint?'

Flourishing his paint brush triumphantly, the Doctor marched out of the control room.

Leela knelt down and kissed K9 on the end of his nose.

DOCTOR WHO

0426114558	TERRANCE DICKS **Doctor Who and The** **Abominable Snowmen**	£1.35
0426200373	**Doctor Who and The** **Android Invasion**	£1.25
0426201086	**Doctor Who and The** **Androids of Tara**	£1.25
0426116313	IAN MARTER **Doctor Who and The** **Ark in Space**	£1.25
0426201043	TERRANCE DICKS **Doctor Who and The** **Armageddon Factor**	£1.25
0426112954	**Doctor Who and The** **Auton Invasion**	£1.50
0426116747	**Doctor Who and The** **Brain of Morbius**	£1.35
0426110250	**Doctor Who and The** **Carnival of Monsters**	£1.25
042611471X	MALCOLM HULKE **Doctor Who and** **The Cave Monsters**	£1.50
0426117034	TERRANCE DICKS **Doctor Who and The** **Claws of Axos**	£1.35
042620123X	DAVID FISHER **Doctor Who and The** **Creature from the Pit**	£1.25
0426113160	DAVID WHITAKER **Doctor Who and The Crusaders**	£1.50
0426200616	BRIAN HAYLES **Doctor Who and The Curse** **of Peladon**	£1.50
0426114639	GERRY DAVIS **Doctor Who and The Cybermen**	£1.50
0426113322	BARRY LETTS **Doctor Who and The Daemons**	£1.50

Prices are subject to alteration

DOCTOR WHO

0426101103	DAVID WHITAKER **Doctor Who and The Daleks**	**£1.50**
042611244X	TERRANCE DICKS **Doctor Who and The Dalek Invasion of Earth**	**£1.25**
0426103807	**Doctor Who and The Day of the Daleks**	**£1.35**
042620042X	**Doctor Who – Death to the Daleks**	**£1.35**
0426119657	**Doctor Who and The Deadly Assassin**	**£1.25**
0426200969	**Doctor Who and The Destiny of the Daleks**	**£1.35**
0426108744	MALCOLM HULKE **Doctor Who and The Dinosaur Invasion**	**£1.35**
0426103726	**Doctor Who and The Doomsday Weapon**	**£1.35**
0426201464	IAN MARTER **Doctor Who and The Enemy of the World**	**£1.25**
0426200063	TERRANCE DICKS **Doctor Who and The Face of Evil**	**£1.25**
0426201507	ANDREW SMITH **Doctor Who – Full Circle**	**£1.35**
0426112601	TERRANCE DICKS **Doctor Who and The Genesis of the Daleks**	**£1.35**
0426112792	**Doctor Who and The Giant Robot**	**£1.25**
0426115430	MALCOLM HULKE **Doctor Who and The Green Death**	**£1.35**

Prices are subject to alteration

DOCTOR WHO

	TERRANCE DICKS	
0426200330	Doctor Who and The **Hand of Fear**	£1.25
0426201310	Doctor Who and The **Horns of Nimon**	£1.25
0426200098	Doctor Who and The **Horror of Fang Rock**	£1.25
0426108663	BRIAN HAYLES Doctor Who and The **Ice Warriors**	£1.35
0426200772	Doctor Who and The **Image of the Fendahl**	£1.25
0426200934	TERRANCE DICKS Doctor Who and The **Invasion of Time**	£1.35
0426200543	Doctor Who and The **Invisible Enemy**	£1.25
0426201485	Doctor Who and The **Keeper of Traken**	£1.35
0426201256	PHILIP HINCHCLIFFE Doctor Who and The **Keys of Marinus**	£1.35
0426201477	DAVID FISHER Doctor Who and The **Leisure Hive**	£1.25
0426110412	TERRANCE DICKS Doctor Who and The **Loch Ness Monster**	£1.25
0426201493	CHRISTOPHER H BIDMEAD **Doctor Who – Logopolis**	£1.25
0426118936	PHILIP HINCHCLIFFE Doctor Who and The **Masque of Mandragora**	£1.25
0426201329	TERRANCE DICKS Doctor Who and The **Monster of Peladon**	£1.25

Prices are subject to alteration

STAR Books are obtainable from many booksellers and newsagents. If you have any difficulty please send purchase price plus postage on the scale below to:-

Star Cash Sales
P.O. Box 11
Falmouth
Cornwall
OR
Star Book Service,
G.P.O. Box 29,
Douglas,
Isle of Man,
British Isles.

While every effort is made to keep prices low, it is sometimes necessary to increase prices at short notice. Star Books reserve the right to show new retail prices on covers which may differ from those advertised in the text or elsewhere.

Postage and Packing Rate
UK: 45p for the first book, 20p for the second book and 14p for each additional book ordered to a maximum charge of £1.63. BFPO and EIRE: 45p for the first book, 20p for the second book, 14p per copy for the next 7 books thereafter 8p per book. Overseas: 75p for the first book and 21p per copy for each additional book.